TANG'S CHRISTMAS MIRACLE

A Love Story for Pet Lovers

Daphne Lynn Stewart

Copyright © 2023 Daphne Lynn Stewart

All rights reserved

The characters and events portrayed in this book are fictitious. Any similarity to real persons, living or dead, is coincidental and not intended by the author.

No part of this book may be reproduced, or stored in a retrieval system, or transmitted in any form or by any means, electronic, mechanical, photocopying, recording, or otherwise, without express written permission of the publisher.

ISBN-13: 9798864185407

Cover design by: Deborah Cannon

Printed in the United States of America

For Aubrey

CHAPTER 1

Sometimes bad things happen before good things can. Jonny has been telling me this for years, ever since Mom and Dad divorced. I find it hard to believe. Nothing could be worse than what I just learned today. On top of that, Christmas was coming. I should be thinking about special gifts for my family, spicy gingerbread and rum-soaked fruitcake and where to get an organic turkey.

I can't even think about the holidays. My head is filled with worry. And I know what Jonny would say. He is pragmatic. And while he is my brother and never wants me to be unhappy, can he really understand how I feel?

Can Mom? I wish she were here so I could ask her.

Oh, why do bad things happen around the holidays?

That was when the family cat ran away, I got

braces, and my parents decided to call it quits. Each of these awful events happened around Christmas.

Dad remarried and moved to Europe ten years ago. We never see him anymore. Mom is in Toronto. Jonny is in Vancouver. My brother and I split the holidays between his house and Mom's every other year. This year, Christmas is with Jonny's family.

Like him I live in Vancouver, so I won't have to travel this time. Not for Christmas. I work in the pet food industry selling the latest products to corporate chains and local mom and pop shops. The latter are being squeezed out by the bigwigs, but being a pet lover and mom to an adorable shih-poo, my heart goes out to the small businesses. My dream? To own one. I'll call it Miracle Pet Boutique.

Meanwhile there is Tang.

My dog is the happiest dog on earth. I am not kidding. Not only is he friendly, he is sincere. Whenever we go for a walk, he stops to greet every dog, cat, squirrel and person we meet. All people —young and old, babies in strollers and people in wheelchairs—are heroes in his books. He is partial to Canada Post letter carriers—with or without cookies in their pockets.

As he trots along in front of me, he is wagging his tail at everything and nothing at all. Cambie Street, a historic thoroughfare, is lined with quaint shops, coffee places and ethnic restaurants, mostly Asian. We are on our way home from the vet's. He stops to give a young mother dragging a wagon with a toddler inside it a huge howl of joy. A wave of sadness overwhelms me and I almost burst into tears. But this little dude is oblivious to anything but the wonders of being alive.

Like an opera singer, his head tilts up, his snout rises to the heavens dragging out a joyous aria for as long as he can before taking a breath.

At times I swear he is singing.

I would have laughed as my pooch squeezed in between some cedar-frond-filled, concrete planters if not for the threat of tears. Red plastic poinsettias flanked an outdoor patio alongside the planters. His leash had tangled around the fake foliage when he leaped exuberantly at the customer sitting at a table eating what looked like Indian fusion, his enthusiasm so obvious that the customer grinned, unwinding the slack in the leash that had ended up around Tang's neck.

My heart did a flip as the man turned from scratching Tang's floppy ears, and I caught my first glimpse of his stylishly stubbled face. I gasped, "Jonny?"

I climbed over and between the planters to see.

I did so need a friendly face to talk to. But the fact that the man was dressed in a fisherman knit sweater and unzipped down vest should have been my first clue.

Tang, disheveled as usual, rose to his hindquarters and tried to scale up his knees.

Amusement touched the man's lips, and I

clapped a hand to my mouth. The shih-poo, realizing the man's scent was all wrong, obeyed my tug at his leash and returned to his haunches. His fluffy gray tail, though, never stopped whacking the ground.

At first glance, I had been fooled too. Even now, I had to do a doubletake just to be sure. But he was younger than Jonny.

"Oh, I'm afraid we've made a mistake—" I mumbled. "I thought you were somebody else."

Truly, I had thought he was Jonny. Although he couldn't be. Jonny was a busy doctor at the University of British Columbia. The hospital was clear across town. There was no way he could take the time to come this far for lunch. And even if he had, why would he be alone?

"It's okay," the man said. "I have one of those faces. Everyone thinks I'm their brother or uncle or father. Good thing I've never been mistaken for somebody's husband... How would I explain this?" He indicated the delicious-looking, yellow curry on... oysters? That remained on his plate. Then tapped his chest.

Some of the sauce had dripped on the white fisherman knit.

"Curry is a pain to get out," I said.

"Yeah, the wife would be pretty miffed."

A startled pause on my part, and a twinkle of merriment on his. "No wife. I was speaking hypothetically."

I twinkled in turn. He had a way of making me forget my troubles.

My levity vanished, and his expression softened. "Something I said? I didn't mean that only wives did laundry. Bad attempt at humor. *I* do laundry. Every weekend in fact."

He was stumbling unnecessarily. I managed to grin. "No-no, of course not. I'm not offended by anything you said…"

We both fell silent. "Are you okay?" he asked after a moment.

A tear slipped down my cheek and I wiped it away. "Yes. Yes, I'm fine." I went to pull my dog and his muddy paws off the nice man's knees.

"I'm so sorry about that." I unwrapped the knitted scarf from my neck to brush away the smudge on his pants and only succeeded in catching the scarf in my earring, which tugged painfully at my earlobe, nearly ripping my ear.

"Whoa, whoa, whoa," he said, as I stood helplessly, neck craning, head tilted, weighed down by the scarf, trying to avoid more damage, mittened fingers useless as I couldn't see where I was caught in the loops. And only succeeded in getting my wool mittens snagged too.

"Let me help you with that." He rose and I realized he was even taller than Jonny. He had to bend down to help unhook my Silver Bell earring from my accessories, much to my chagrin.

My face was now the color of my scarf.

"Those are nice earrings."

"Thank you," I said, completely disarmed.

"Very pretty, and very festive... How's the ear?"

"The ear is fine. No damage. Thanks to you."

Tang wished to show his gratitude too and threw his dirty wet paws on the man's knees.

I grabbed the hanging end of my scarf, now with a long snag in it, and tried to brush away the dirt even as I yanked Tang back.

He waved me away. "Goes with the curry. Almost Art Deco, don't you think?" His laugh was contagious. "Don't worry about it. I'll change when I get back to my hotel."

"Your hotel? You're from out of town?"

He nodded and resumed his seat. "I'm here for a conference." His breath puffed, and his chin tipped towards the snowy peaks of the North Shore Mountains and the icy waters of False Creek. A bridge, lined in Christmas banners, funneled the speeding traffic downtown. There, steel and glass office towers, hotels and businesses crowded the scene.

What kind of conference? I crushed the urge to ask. We were strangers.

By this time, I was beginning to realize I was monopolizing his time. If here for a conference, he would want to get back after finishing his lunch. At this rate he would never get finished.

I might have thought it strange him eating outside in December, but since the pandemic, restaurants had invested in heated patios. There was an adobe-style gaslit firepit at one end of the stone patio, and he was one of three customers who had decided to dine *al fresco*. The scene was cozy. The damp air seeped into your bones however if you stopped moving. So, although it wasn't odd to see someone eating outdoors in winter, what did strike me as odd was to see an attractive man dining alone. Especially since he was so sociable.

The wind was cold; a definite nip in the air. Traffic was heavy and sluggish due to multiple stoplights at the intersections. Horns honked and birds chirped and a vapour was rising from the road. People in running shoes, sweatpants and hoodies, clutching umbrellas or wearing raingear strolled past. He had a misty ringside seat to all of this.

"Being with colleagues all day, *every* day, for five days can be a bit much," he said by way of apology.

"No need to explain. It's none of my business."

I gathered up the leash with both mitted hands as my shih-poo leaped up again, tail in motion. I coiled the slack in my right fist and insisted he sit. He ignored me. And continued to dance around. "Tang tends to get carried away."

The man smiled. "A very friendly dog. What was his name?"

"Tang."

"Tang? What a great name... As in the dynasty? Or as in the dehydrated orange drink that the astronauts took into space in the 1960s...? Either way, I love it."

I grinned. "As in the dynasty."

"Somehow it suits him."

"Thanks."

But Tang hardly looked like an emperor's dog. He had fluffy, but somewhat scruffy fur and it was hand cut by *moi*. When he was a puppy, his hair was jet black with white mutton chops, a bright white patch on his chest, and a single white paw. After his first haircut, his downy undercoat appeared, a soft dove gray. I'd had to change his description at the city licensing department from 'black & white' to 'gray & white'.

"He—we—thought you were my brother," I explained. "You look a lot like him. Except for the way you're dressed. I don't think Jonny would be caught dead in a crewneck sweater. Not that there's anything wrong with crewnecks. It's just not his taste. It's a V-neck or nothing." I paused realizing I was babbling. "Or eating oysters for that matter..."

"No problem." He extended a hand. There was no awkwardness on his side. "I'm Joel Joseph. A bit of a mouthful, I know, but that's my name."

"Pleased to meet you. My name is Marilee. Marilee Christian. But my friends call me Mari."

"Pleased to meet you, Marilee." Joel flashed me his wicked smile, then lowered his head to Tang and scratched him under the chin. "Definitely pleased to meet *you*, happy dude."

Tang responded by wagging his tail furiously and releasing a longwinded happy bark, ending the note with a high-pitched twist.

Joel grinned. "The feeling is mutual."

His kindness towards me and Tang was lifting my spirits. But then he said the strangest thing.

"It's bad news, isn't it."

My eyes widened in surprise. What was he talking about?

Joel was now holding Tang's head in his hands and examining his front teeth. A tooth had been removed from his lower left jaw along with a suspicious mass. In their place was a couple of stitches, nearly dissolved.

Speechless, as Joel glanced up at me, I dropped to my knees and cupped my boy to my chest. When I first got Tang five years ago, I had no idea it was possible to love a pet so much.

I nodded my head and the tears spilled.

"It's all right, Marilee. There is treatment for his condition."

How did he know? Was he psychic?

The scarf I had used to wipe at the mud smears Tang had left on Joel's pants was now my handkerchief. I nodded as I mopped up the tears. The vet told me the best way to save Tang's life was to fly him to the Ontario Veterinary College hospital in Guelph.

He said that Tang was a trooper. But trooper or not, I was terrified to proceed. How was Tang going to eat? What would he look like with his jaw partially removed? What if the cancer had spread? Was it worth putting Tang through all this pain and suffering just so I could have him a little while longer? Was I being selfish? I did not want Tang to suffer.

The waiter came at that moment and Joel took out his credit card to pay for his lunch. He glanced at his phone and noted the time. "I've got to go or I'll be late. I'm giving a paper in just over an hour and I've got to change."

"Wait, Joel," I pleaded. I felt desperate. I needed to know more. I felt guilty for detaining him, but my desperation overrode the guilt.

He nodded sympathetically. "These cases are rare but treatable. In fact, that's why I'm in Vancouver. The Canadian Veterinary Medical Association is having their annual meeting to present new findings in feline and canine Cancer research." He paused. "I'm a veterinary surgeon."

My head shot up at that.

Then there really was hope!

CHAPTER 2

Tang expresses his love of life in a very vocal way. He has a special greeting where he raises his head to the sky and howls happily. Translated from dog language it means, "Joy to the World!"

Dinner was at my brother's place tonight. Eva, his wife, was cooking. They had two kids, fraternal twins, a boy and a girl. They were at that age where their relationship had become love-hate. Boys will be boys, but girls just wanna have fun—that was what Eva would say. At age six, the only things they agreed on was that Christmas was a wonder, and that Tang was their favorite dog.

It was Jonny's fortieth birthday and I had promised to attend.

As soon as we walked in the door Tang burst into song at the sight of the kids at the TV. Michael and Mia jumped up to greet him and he climbed up their legs eager to give kisses. They raced him back to the large-screen TV to finish watching their favorite streaming cartoon.

Mom had introduced them to the original animated series, *Casper the Friendly Ghost* last year. The soundtrack was currently playing. It always made me think of Tang and obviously it made the twins think of him too. They were both singing at the top of their lungs:

"Tang, Tang the friendly dog,
The friendliest dog we know....
He always says hello,
He's really glad to meet you.
Wherever he may go,
He's kind to every living creature..."

I mustn't show the kids how emotional I felt. I didn't want to ruin Jonny's birthday party.

I hugged the twins where they sat playing with Tang in front of the TV. Then went to the kitchen to greet their mother.

Jonny and Eva lived in Arbutus Village, an upscale neighborhood, centrally located in Vancouver's westside. Their house was modern contemporary with floor to ceiling windows in the kitchen/family room and also in the living area. These were currently all decked out in multicolored festive lights and shiny red and green garlands.

The style was open concept and the kids were visible in the family room while Eva prepared dinner at the quartz counter.

"Hi Marilee," she said, raising the knife she held in salutation. She was chopping cucumbers and tomatoes for a salad. "Did you remember to pick up the cake?"

"I did," I said and set the cakebox on the counter beside some sliced radishes and mushrooms. "Does it need to go in the fridge?"

"Did you just pick it up?"

I nodded.

"Then probably not. The fridge is completely full right now."

I opened the double doors of the extra capacity stainless steel refrigerator and noted the lack of available space. Every inch of the glass shelves and drawers was laden with food, some already prepared and arranged on platters.

Eva was one of those people who loved to entertain. She also loved to cook and bake. And her stuffed refrigerator and plumpish figure were a delightful testimony to that.

"Can you take those canapés out for me, Marilee?" she asked.

I removed the platters of smoked salmon blinis and goat cheese cranberry tarts.

"Is Jonny not home yet?"

"He texted twenty minutes ago that he was on his way... Oh, here he is now."

The back door opened and Jonny came in from the flagstone patio, carrying the cold air with him.

He shut out the winter and the warmth of central heating wrapped around me.

I waved at my brother with the hand that wasn't stuffing canapés into my mouth. I realized now since I'd received the bad news that I had forgotten to eat all day.

Jonny kissed Eva on the cheek, and gave me his half wave. *She* was what he meant all those times he'd told me that sometimes bad things had to happen before good things could. Eva was his second wife. The first marriage was to his college sweetheart. It was no one's fault he insisted. They had just married too young and then grew apart.

This marriage however was the real thing. Eva was an executive hospital administrator. When she had the twins, she decided to take a hiatus from her job to raise them. The wonder of it all was that both she and Jonny knew what they wanted and were willing to help each other acquire their dreams. I hoped one day that would happen for me. I had lousy taste in men. Chose poorly every time. While Eva was taking a hiatus from her job, I was taking a hiatus from dating. My number one concern now was my dog. Even my job had taken a backseat.

"Happy birthday, Bro," I said, wiping my fingers discreetly on my skinny, distressed jeans.

"Thanks, Mari. Glad you could make it for dinner."

Before he could even remove his gloves and winter coat, Michael and Mia came scrambling up to climb all over him. They were the second good thing that had followed after his first marriage had fallen apart.

The way they loved their dad always made me smile. When they were done tearing his limbs apart with love tugs, he went into the front foyer to stow away his winter gear.

"Dinner is in half an hour," Eva called as he left the kitchen. She turned to me, pointing to the platters inside the opened fridge. "Take those canapés into the family room, and here, take these too." She shoved some snowman napkins at me, and I moved everything into the family room. The kids flocked over to grab a snack and I went to see my brother, Tang following behind me.

As soon as Tang saw Jonny he gave a tremendous howl of joy, making my brother laugh. This had the effect of causing me to crumple into tears.

"Hey, what's the matter?" He finished hanging his coat and stuffing his gloves onto a shelf above the coat rack.

Jonny was not a demonstrative man when it came to his sister, but when it came to his children, they were his pride and joy. With hugs and kisses all around.

"Sorry, Jonny," I whimpered. "I'm just not myself today."

"What happened?"

"It can wait. It's your birthday."

"I'll have another one next year. My birthday is nothing." Just because he wasn't a hugger with me, that didn't mean he wasn't perceptive. He led me into his study and sat me down on the sofa. "Now talk. What happened."

How to begin? My life was falling apart.

"It's Tang."

Tang was wagging his tail at the family cat who was sprawled on the top of Jonny's overstuffed recliner. Tang loved cats. And dogs. And people. He didn't differentiate when it came to spreading the love. And Emily was his favorite feline. I don't think the feeling was mutual. Emily rolled onto her back, dismissing the pesky mutt as though he wasn't even there.

"What happened at the vet?" he asked.

I gulped. My answer barely came out. "It's cancer. Just below his lower left canine."

Tang came over to be patted as my brother sat down beside me. He stroked Tang's head.

I knew what he wanted to say; it was nature's way. But if it was a person, he would do everything in his power to treat the disease. He was a doctor after all.

"What did the vet say?"

"He suggests, if it is at all possible, that I take him to Ontario where there are specialists. He has the best chance there. BC has no facilities quite as sophisticated. The Ontario Veterinary College actually has an Animal Cancer Center."

"But you hate flying."

"It's Tang. I have to do it." And I had ways of managing. The flying part, I mean.

"And how much will it cost?"

"The cost doesn't matter. I'll pay it."

Jonny lifted Tang onto his lap. Tang had no idea there was anything wrong. He wasn't in pain. The vet had removed the tooth last week and taken a biopsy of the tumor beneath it. The prognosis was bad. Without treatment, he would die.

"How soon?"

"Soon. I have to leave in the next couple of days. I've already booked our flight. The only problem is my job. My boss won't give me the time off. I have a special account that I have to win and the meeting is in four days. But I can't postpone until after the meeting. I can't wait that long. Tang can't wait. And the boss won't even consider changing the date."

I feared I was completely incoherent but I continued: "The OVC hospital has a spot open on the same day as the meeting. If I don't take it, it could be days or even weeks before a cancellation and another opening is available. Tang could die. So, I booked the spot. But my boss insists that the client can't be asked to reschedule for my dog."

"Maybe *I* can reschedule then. I will take Tang to this hospital."

I burst into tears again. My brother would do that for me? But how could I ask that of him? He was a doctor. His patients needed him. "You know you can't do that, Jonny. Not if you want to take time off for Christmas. You have cancer patients of your own."

Asking Eva was out of the question. I knew she would help if she could, but there were the twins.

I swallowed the lump in my throat and choked on a sniffle. "I'll just have to find another job when I get back."

"Your boss won't budge?"

I shook my head. "I told Mr. Hancock after the surgery, I would fly back leaving Tang at the hospital, do the presentation, and then fly back. The vet told me Tang would be in the hospital for three days. I pleaded with Mr. Hancock. But he said no. What if there were complications and I couldn't return? And he doubted that they would allow me to leave the dog without a contact person nearby." I gulped nearly choking with emotion. "If I don't take that meeting, I'm fired. He said it wasn't personal, that I was his best executive rep. But if I failed to show up for the meeting and make my presentation, I wasn't the right kind of person for the job."

I sighed. "Maybe he's right. Maybe I am not the right kind of person for this job."

"Nonsense. You've worked so hard. You're at the top of your profession. No one has a better sales record than you." He paused to think. "What about Mom? She's in Toronto. That's not so far away from Guelph, is it?"

About an hour and a half drive. But Mom was also a busy doctor. In fact, she was Chief of Surgery at the Sunnybrook Health Sciences Hospital. Could I do that to her?

No. No, I could not.

I would have to go myself. Tang was *my* dog. I was his mom. I couldn't bear being away from him anyways. Not with a condition as serious as his.

He needed me. I would not let my boy down. I would spend as much time as was needed to see him through in Guelph. I would make a terrible pitch anyways if I was worrying about Tang. And I *would* be. Every moment that we were apart I would be worrying. I *had* to be there. If it cost me my job, so be it. Tang was worth it.

"Dinner is ready!" Eva called from the kitchen.

I was ashamed of myself for putting a damper on Jonny's birthday party. I should have kept the news to myself until tomorrow. But he shook it off. "There is nothing more important than family," he said. "And Tang is family."

Tang who was still sitting on my brother's lap, rose to his hind quarters and started licking Jonny's face. Who says dogs aren't smart?

After a delicious dinner of prime rib roast, sweet potatoes, salad and stir-fried bok choy, we had vanilla-orange cake and ice cream, and retired to the family room.

Three weeks before Christmas and the tree was already up. It felt a little more like a Christmas party than a birthday party. That was the problem with being born so close to the holidays.

It was the twin's bedtime and they were bickering over which toy they were going to take to bed. Funny how kids wanted the same thing their brother or sister wanted. In this case it was a white curly, lamb stuffie. Yesterday, Eva said, it was a stuffed Yeti. They had toys galore and no matter how many toys their parents bought them, they always wanted the exact same one. Was this a twin thing? A sibling thing? Or merely a kid thing?

Eva once even tried giving the twins the identical toy so they wouldn't fight over it, but they ignored the copies. Nope, I think it was more like puppy behavior. The toy was not special if it was duplicated.

Tang was about to solve the conflict by taking the stuffie for himself when I promised to read them a story if they stopped squabbling over the lamb.

This they agreed on. I settled them on the sofa, with me in the middle and Tang curled up in Mia's lap. Needless to say, I did not mention Tang's condition to them. Pointless to worry them until the surgery was done, and I had all the facts concerning his recovery.

"What do you want me to read?" I asked.

Michael piped up. "The Story of Christmas!"

He had an illustrated hardcover book of the traditional Christmas tale, and slid it onto my lap. It was one of those Little Golden Books, that Mom used to buy us when we were kids. They were first published in 1944 and the company continues to publish new stories today. With 1144 titles to their credit, they tackle every topic in the world.

Jonny must have continued the tradition with his own kids. So... they wanted to read the Christmas Story.... I am not particularly religious, but for the first time in my life I truly hoped there was a God.

I picked up the book and turned the page. It was the classic tale of the birth of Jesus. How Mary and Joseph had gone to Bethlehem so that they could register for the King's census. The couple found that there were no vacancies at any of the inns and so they stayed in the stables where Mary's baby boy was born.

I don't remember all the details of this story. Except that a brilliant star—the Star of Bethlehem—appeared in the sky. And sparked wonder across the world.

The angels spread the word about the new king and the shepherds came with their flocks by night. And three wisemen brought frankincense, gold and myrrh.

To this day I do not know what frankincense and myrrh are. Gold yes. Or why a baby, divine or otherwise, would require such things.

But no matter. That was how the story went. And it almost brought tears to my eyes but I laughed through them until I reached the happy ending when this baby—the baby Jesus—lay in a manger in swaddling clothes surrounded by sheep, donkeys and goats, while admirers came from far and wide bearing gifts.

This edition did not tell of King Herod's evil plan. Kill every first-born son in Bethlehem to be certain that Mary's son was eliminated, ensuring Jesus could never take Herod's place as king. Such a tale was not appropriate for six-year-olds.

When I finished, Eva told the twins it was time for bed. Each was allowed to take one toy to sleep with. And Michael and Mia started fighting over the stuffed toy lamb again.

I said calmly, "What did we just read?"

Mia glanced at me. Then at her brother. "Okay, you can have Lambchop tonight. If I can sleep with him tomorrow night."

Michael agreed.

The Christmas Story evoked one important message. Love one another.

I smiled at Tang as he climbed from one lap to the other, tail thwacking away. And gave goodnight kisses all around.

Love one another. That was Tang's missive too.

CHAPTER 3

Tang was used to me leaving him with Eva when I went to work. He and she took the kids to school and then he spent the day watching Eva bake Christmas cookies, taking a snooze every now and then when the goodies didn't turn out to be for him.

I almost took him to work with me this morning instead of dropping him off at my brother's. I had to try to convince my boss one more time. This time in person.

Maybe if he actually met Tang, he'd have a change of heart. But I decided it could just as easily put him off.

That left me few options. If Mr. Hancock forbade me to go to Guelph to save my dog's life, I had no choice but to quit. My flight was in two days. Tang's surgery was scheduled at the OVC hospital the day after our arrival.

I worked at headquarters in the downtown

office of the largest petfood company in North America—National Pet. The building was a massive glass and steel tower that represented the kind of image the corporation wished to evoke. All encompassing, omnipresent. A household name.

We were pushing a new organic brand of high-end dog food to compete with the smaller artisanal brands that were popping up all over the country. People loved their dogs as much as they loved their children. In fact, to many folks, their pups *were* their children. And only the best was good enough. Generic commercial pet food fell short.

My job was to convince the big chain pet stores to stock our brand.

The meeting that Mr. Hancock wanted me to pitch was for EveryPet Emporium, the top pet store chain in the nation. I had to convince him that one of my colleagues could do the pitch. I would give them my PowerPoint presentation and all of my notes and research.

Made with fresh meat. No by-products. Only organic fruits and vegetables. No additives, no dyes, no chemicals. No sprayed-on flavorings or color. Pure and natural goodness.

A tough sell because everyone was doing it.

But that was the least of my problems at the moment.

As I strolled out of the elevator rehearsing my speech, my assistant Sarah Phipps, came towards me from the direction of Mr. Hancock's office. The office opened at 8:00am and most of the execs arrived before that. What was she doing here so early? She wasn't required to be.

No clues to be found since everyone had their heads turned to their computers and their glass doors shut. Only the CEO (Chief Executive Officer), the CFO (Chief Financial Officer), the CMO (Chief Marketing Officer) and the COO (Chief Operations Officer) had offices up here.

"Oh, you've arrived," she said before I could ask. "He's expecting you."

But who was expecting her? What was she doing on the penthouse floor? Her job level was two down from mine. Even I was rarely invited upstairs.

"I have some papers for you to sign off on," she said, patting the densely-typed printouts in her hand.

There was something different about her behavior this morning. She was strangely self-confident and not afraid to flaunt it. Did something happen? Was she promoted? There was talk among the higher ups that she was in line for a bump up, but they seldom made those decisions, especially when it concerned one of my team, without my involvement. And I had heard nothing about a promotion for her from the bigwigs.

I shrugged and forced a happy face. "Leave them on my desk. And while you're at it, I have a PowerPoint I want you to review. It's on my laptop. Have you looked at it yet?"

"On it, boss," she said.

"Thanks. And please make sure you know it inside out. This might be the most important meeting of your life."

"Sure, boss." She sent me a very self-satisfied smile. "See you downstairs."

I reacted with a nod. Still puzzled, I went to the big glass doors beyond the penthouse lobby and the Chief Executive Officer's private secretary's big glass desk, all the while wondering: What the heck was she doing in the CEO's office?

"But Mr. Hancock," I pleaded as I sat across from him in his penthouse office. The room had a private executive washroom and a library. I could see the tempered glass cases of books past the glass doors. In fact, two thirds of this office had floor to ceiling windows, and outside someone was on a platformed boom, harnessed for safety, washing those windows with a power squeegee and a sloshing, soapy, industrial sized bucket.

The air here held a taint of cigar smoke and something else. Whiskey? Since when was Mr. Hancock a cigar smoker or whiskey drinker at—I glanced at the phone in my hand—at 8:15 in the morning? This meeting was deliberately scheduled before the day's events could interfere.

He had a massive glass and chrome desk

containing a brushed nickel name plate with ebony lettering that read:

Magnus H. Hancock
CEO and President

There was no sign of a smoking cigar or an opened whiskey bottle. Or a glass to accompany it.

"Sarah has helped me with the research," I insisted, observing for any reaction to the name. "She's willing to do the presentation."

"Sarah has six months experience to your nine years," Mr. Hancock said. I was surprised that he even knew who Sarah was, no less how long she'd been with the firm. He barely knew who *I* was. "In that time, how often has she accompanied you on a sales call?"

Once.

I almost lied and told him: 'Multiple times.' But her job description was as my assistant. She was not a sales representative and she had next to no field experience. While she was bright and anxious to learn she had never handled an account before.

Although I was going to bat for her, I couldn't help wondering once again, what she was doing on this floor.

When I was a simple sales assistant, before I was promoted to sales representative and long before I was bumped up to executive sales, which was just one below Chief Marketing Officer, I was never called to this floor. Rumor said I was up for the job of CMO when the current holder of the title retired. And then I would get an office up here. Back in my early days, I knew no one on this floor, not even the administrators or their assistants. Now I pretty much recognized everyone, although I still had no reason to come up to the penthouse very often.

The tenor of his voice changed as though he had noticed my mental detour. And that brought me out of my musings and back to the discussion.

"...Especially not one this large or this important," Mr. Hancock was saying. "Please, believe me, Marilee. I understand your concern for your pet. After all, we're in the business. But I need you. If we lose this account. Well... there will be repercussions. There could be layoffs. Restructuring."

His dark eyes were uncompromising and I knew I had lost this round. "Make other arrangements. Please."

How to get him to empathize? I tried to explain how the best veterinary surgeons and facilities were in Guelph. That this really was a matter of life and death.

The conversation had started out friendly and calm, but it was quickly escalating to something else. Impatience was trembling in his voice, and he was close to exasperation.

"I am not telling you *not* to send your dog there.

I am telling you to delay the surgery or even ask a friend or family member to take your dog for you. You can fly out there after the presentation."

How could I do that? My family had obligations. And if I delayed the surgery Tang could die. Time was of the essence. Tang was a young dog, just five years old. The cancer was growing fast. Every day counted.

And how could I send him with someone else even if there was someone who was able and willing to go? He needed me.

"It's only another three days," Mr. Hancock said, growing querulous. He wore an impatient expression on his face that said: 'It's only an animal.'

"In three days is the exact day the surgery is scheduled."

"And that is when the meeting is. The date is firm. I'm sorry."

He stood up, the signal for me to go.

I rose, miserably. Why was he being so unreasonable? Surely anyone with a heart could see how vital this was to me? Did Mr. Hancock not have a compassionate bone in his body?

Here he was, one of the wealthiest men in the country and he couldn't see it in his heart to give me some slack?

"I know I seem hard to you, Marilee. But everyone has pets and family members who get sick or... or have some other important issue that needs to be dealt with. Yes, we have compassion days for those incidences provided they fit the criteria. It's in the union rules. Your job is different. You are an executive. You get paid to make certain sacrifices. It's in your job description." He fiddled with an open file on his desk; the papers were all askew. He looked as though he wished to tear them up. Which made me realize they were important.

Was it something I could help him with?

I started to speak when he noticed my distraction. The print was tiny and it was impossible to read anything upside down. The only thing I took note of was that some of those lines required signatures. He gathered the papers quickly into a pile before I could surmise anything further, and shoved the lot inside the folder and clapped it shut.

So, nothing he wanted my opinion on.

Message received. He had work to do and was wasting valuable moments talking to me. His impatience travelled from his hands to his eyes. He released the file and raised his head to the door.

His office was spacious. It was a long walk from here to there. He accompanied me to the exit, not something he did routinely.

"There are ways to deal with your problem and still have a successful outcome. None of this is personal. I am not making your life difficult on purpose. You chose to accept the promotion. You knew what responsibilities came with it. Hire someone to take your dog to the special hospital if you have no friend or family member who can do it."

I was silent. Everything he said made sense.

But not to me.

He stopped when we arrived at the door. He was standing close to me and I could definitely smell the cigar and whiskey. The sliding glass doors automatically opened as we neared.

"Thank you for your time, Mr. Hancock," I murmured and stepped through.

"I expect to see you at the company Christmas party," he said to my back. "Don't disappoint me."

CHAPTER 4

I had a good mind to bail; I was much too upset. But it was one of my duties as a sales executive. Mr. Hancock wanted to make a good showing, hence all of his Christmas parties included invites to employees in all departments, their families and even those who had well-behaved pets.

Maybe this was another chance to convince him. I would bring Tang.

The Christmas party was semi-formal. But as an executive I was expected to arrive in more formal attire. I think that was stipulated in the executive handbook to discourage executives from bringing their young toddlers and pets. No one would say it directly. It would seem contradictory. But for once in my life, I was going to bend the rules.

My fashion sense is somewhat retro. Or vintage. I prefer tailored, fitted looks. When styles got looser, I started looking in vintage shops for clothes. The dress I selected for tonight was a 1960's off-shoulder, velvet, bodycon dress. It was stunning in dark green with a tapered waist and a tulip skirt that came to the knee. I wore it with several silver chains in varying lengths, and the Silver Bell earrings that dangled from several chain-links of their own. It was no wonder the bell had caught in my scarf.

It brought a smile as the memory of me and Joel playing Twister with my earring and scarf returned. He'd been so firm, yet gentle. What a great surgeon he must be.

Jonny called just as I was getting ready. He offered to puppysit while I was at the party. I told him that this year I was taking Tang as my plus one. Tang's ensemble was a simple bright red bowtie over a dark green collar.

"You positive that's a good idea?" he asked. "I'm sure the twins would love to have him for the evening."

"Thanks, Jonny. But no thanks. Some people bring their pets—if they're well behaved. Tang is always well behaved. And I want Tang at the party."

"But I thought—"

"You thought wrong. Tang is invited."

"Okay. Have fun."

I intended to have more than fun.

Many of National Pet's clients were invited to the party. That meant there was a chance the CPO in charge of purchasing for the EveryPet franchise would be there.

I squeezed my toes into my black stilettoes. In the business world height mattered. I wasn't particularly tall, so every inch counted. Heels would help to catch their attention. And have the VIP's talking to my face instead of the top of my head.

I had no idea if the Chief Purchasing Officer for EveryPet Emporium was a man or a woman. But what difference would that make? I took a moment to peruse as I wiggled into my white faux fur coat. Come to think of it, maybe it would matter. Women tended to be more sympathetic than men.

I stumbled over to my computer and turned it on. I was about to do a search, then realized that Sarah would know more about this than I did. I had assigned her most of the research after Tang's diagnosis of cancer.

I glanced at the time. Sarah might still be at home. Or I could catch her en route to the party. The phone rang and she answered after the third ring.

"Hi boss, what's up?" she asked.

"Sarah, are you still at home?"

"No. I'm on the road. At a stoplight. I've got you on speakerphone."

"This won't take a second, but hang up if the light changes. I have a question for you. It concerns Les Malt."

Suddenly, it dawned on me how negligent I

had been in the weeks since I found myself in this medical crisis with my pet. How could I not know the sex of my prospective client?

This was the one part of my research I had stupidly neglected, as I had thought the gender of the company's representatives irrelevant. It was absolutely relevant. As I recalled there would be three representatives from that client. The most important one was the CPO. The others were secondary in the hierarchy. Three was the magic number if it came down to a vote. Two against one. I had to get those two votes.

"I'm sorry for bothering you while you're driving, Sarah. But just quickly. Is the CPO for EveryPet Emporium a—ah—?" I felt really stupid for asking. I should already know. The Chief Purchasing Officer was named Les Malt. Short for Leslie? Lester? I had arrogantly assumed it was a man. I forced the words out. "Is the CPO male or female. Or…?"

The phone I had tucked into my purse suddenly dinged. Sarah really was a fantastic assistant. She had quickly Googled the name and texted me a bio with pictures. I saw that he was a she. Fabulous. That upped the odds of getting her understanding. And once she met Tang—

Furthermore, Sarah had sent me the bios of the other reps. Of the other two, one was male and the other female.

Even better.

Two women. One man. That doubled my chances.

"Thanks, Sarah. You are a Godsend."

"No problem."

"Is there anything I can do for you—"

"As a matter of fact, there is," she said.

I wasn't expecting this as people always said that after someone did them a favor. It's not that we were lying. It was just that we didn't expect to have to reciprocate immediately. Of course, I would repay her. That was a given.

I hoped it was something in my power to give.

Sarah was totally oblivious of my hesitation. She went straight to the point and I could just picture her monitoring the traffic, searching the internet and conversing with me on her cell simultaneously, and not once was she flustered. That's how good she was.

"Can I borrow those Silver Bell earrings you wore to work yesterday? I just love them and I think they'd go fabulous with the outfit I'm wearing tonight."

"You want to borrow them tonight?"

"Yes, if that's okay. I mean…"

To be truthful, that was an easy request. And I shouldn't even be thinking about Joel. Because with the mention of the Silver Bell earrings, the chance meeting with Joel replayed in my memory. The incident was embarrassing, so I was humiliated to be reminded of my klutziness. But really, it wasn't that. It was just that he had noticed them when I got one of the bells hooked on my scarf. Oh, what was I doing? I was never going to see him again. Where did he even live?

He was staying in a hotel, so not in town. He never mentioned where he came from, did he?

Why hadn't I asked?

Because that would have been too forward. We had just met. I had just learned that he was a veterinary surgeon. And he knew exactly what Tang's issue was without my having to tell him. He was also in a hurry to get back to his hotel to change for his presentation at the conference.

Good thing it wasn't me that had caused him to drip curry on his sweater.

Though Tang might have had something to do with it.

Oh, dear.

I owed him and had no idea how to get in touch with him. If Tang had caused him to mess up his sweater, that was my fault. I should offer to pay for the dry cleaning.

"Marilee, are you there?" I could hear the roar of a car engine as she stepped on the accelerator. "Would that be okay? Can I borrow your earrings? I've got to go. Light's green."

"I'm sorry, Sarah. I was drifting. I'm so distracted these days."

I'd be an ingrate not to lend her the earrings.

"Sure," I said. "I'll bring them with me."

CHAPTER 5

The party took place at National Pet's headquarters where the main lobby had been transformed into a marble floored, steel and glass ballroom. The white pillars were ribboned in silver, green, and gold. And an enormous thirty-foot Christmas tree decked out in matching colors, and accented with red globes, stood at the far windows. There were also Christmas tree shaped displays of the latest canned pet foods, interspersed with gold and silver bows.

The sweet smells of baked goods and the spiciness of savory treats came from several round, white linen- covered tables with frosted holly and pinecone centerpieces. There was a heady scent of expensive perfumes and men's cologne. Servers dressed in red vests, white shirts and black pants wove between the guests offering hors d'oeuvres on silver platters, and replacing the empty ones on the tables.

Sarah was very visible in her scarlet party dress threaded with black and silver, and black sheer stockings. She was right, these Silver Bells would look stunning with her dress. I removed them from my white clutch when she caught sight of me, and we met in the middle of the floor.

"Thank you so much, boss," she said as I handed the pair of bells to her. She replaced her red button studs with my earrings.

"Matches your silver belt," I said.

"I know. That's why I wanted to borrow them. But I was afraid to ask. Since they're so festive, I thought you might want to wear them yourself tonight."

"Oh, no." I tugged at the silver hoops on my ears. "No. I had planned to wear these all along."

"Great. Oh, look. Mr. Hancock has spotted you. He's coming over. I'll make a quick exit." Before I could stop her, she vanished into the crowd.

It seems he hadn't even noticed Sarah because his focus was on me and my dog.

Mr. Hancock was surprised to see that I had brought Tang, but he was enough of a gentleman not to call me out on my efforts to sway him. He approached before I could think what to say. Tang got a requisite pat, although I suspect, had he met Tang on the street, he would have just walked by. Tang returned the greeting with a howl of joy.

It was unnecessary for Mr. Hancock to voice any objection. The set of his jaw and the steel in his eyes told me Tang's presence was irrelevant. His mind was set.

"And where is Mrs. Hancock, tonight?" I asked, nervously smoothing the velvet of my dress. "I'd like to pay my respects."

I was hoping Natalia was here. Wives had a lot of influence on their husbands, didn't they? Not that I would know, since I was minus husband, and boyfriend.

"Natalia had to fly to Calgary yesterday." His voice was gruff, dismissive. I got the distinct impression he didn't want to discuss her. Then realizing how cold he sounded, he added more gently, "Her mother is ill."

"Oh, I'm sorry to hear that."

"Her mother is ninety."

As though that explained her illness.

"Is it serious?" I asked.

He shrugged.

Message received. It was personal. Although his behavior was weird. And none of my business. I was just an employee. "I hope she gets better soon."

He turned just then as a man approached. For a second, I thought I was hallucinating.

"Joel?" I said, surprised and pleased at the same time. Was I wrong? This time neither Tang nor I mistook him for Jonny. He was dressed in business casual. Khaki pants, a crisp white shirt with collar and a stylish sport coat. No curry stain.

"It's Marilee. Do you remember me?" I asked

hopefully. "We met the other day, on Cambie Street."

He hesitated, and then his face lit up as Tang patted his feet for attention. "Of course. Marilee. You're the woman with the friendly dog." He smiled, and shot a quick look from Tang to my boss. "You work for my father?"

My word! I thought. Mr. Hancock was his father? That told me how little I actually knew about my boss. Granted, Mr. Hancock did not rub shoulders with company employees. In fact, we rarely saw him. Except at specific meetings. "I thought your last name was Joseph."

"It is," he said. "Magnus is my stepfather."

"I see you two know each other," Mr. Hancock said. Then light seemed to dawn in his tightly focused mind, as Magnus Hancock realized the connection. His stepson was a veterinary surgeon, and I was about to use that knowledge to my advantage.

Joel extended a hand. "I'm heading home soon. Just thought I'd stop by and say hello to Magnus and he invited me to this party."

This was wonderful. So what if my intentions came across as manipulative? What choice did I have? This was literally a matter of life and death. I must get Joel to influence his father to allow me the time off to take Tang to Guelph.

"Hello again, little dude," Joel said to the fluffball jumping at his leg.

Mr. Hancock shook his head. Did I say Joel might influence him? Maybe not.

Magnus Hancock and Joel Joseph could not be more different. But then they were unrelated by blood.

Did I detect an eyeroll from the boss? He thought I wasn't looking. But it was clear to me that he thought Joel was paying a little too much attention to my dog. He was squatting, scratching Tang's armpit as Tang raised his right paw.

I glanced up and saw the scowl on Hancock's face. He understood exactly how I was going to use Joel's affection for my dog to serve my needs.

I forced myself to remain calm, and psyched myself up to speak. I needed an ally. And Joel Joseph was the only one who might influence my boss. Joel obviously cared about animals or he wouldn't have become a vet. His stepfather on the other hand. Did he even have a pet? I could honestly say I had never heard Hancock mention a dog or a cat. Or even a bird or goldfish.

Why was Hancock even in the pet business if he didn't care about animals?

Mr. Hancock's curiosity did not extend to how his stepson and I met. I was about to explain the amusing incident when a group of Christmas carolers stopped in front of us dressed like Dickens characters and burst into a refrain of *Hark! The Herald Angels Sing*.

"You should mingle, Marilee," Mr. Hancock said

over the caroling. "There are people here you should meet. Enjoy yourself and Merry Christmas."

Merry Christmas? How could I have a Merry Christmas when he was the reason it wouldn't be?

I swallowed my emotion and felt remorse. That was unfair. Was it his fault that Tang had cancer? No.

He turned his back on me and glanced down to address his stepson who was still playing with Tang. "Joel, I want to introduce you to some people."

I was dismissed. Hancock must get me away from his stepson because he had guessed my nefarious plan.

Joel rose from scratching Tang's rump, sending him into a tailspin of pleasure, and smiled at me. "Hey, good luck with Tang," he said over the song of the carolers who had moved on. And I could see that he sincerely meant it.

"Joel, wait!" I called. But it was too late. The crowd had thickened in the last half hour and Joel had already disappeared behind a group of partyers. "Joel!"

No response. The music and chatter and clinking of glasses and cutlery on plates had drowned my voice.

Every muscle in my body was desperate to run after him, but I had already imposed enough. From what I'd seen in their interaction I was pretty certain that Joel Joseph had little influence on his stepfather. If I could get Joel alone, I could try asking for help. But right now, it was impossible.

The room was an acoustical cacophony of sound. Tang's happy greeting to my colleagues as they came to wish me Happy Holidays was absorbed by all of the noise. Others had brought party-friendly dogs and Tang greeted each in his operatic way. Some of the pooches cocked their heads at what he was doing, especially when he raised his paw like he expected a handshake. He was actually asking for someone to scratch his armpit (I know dogs don't have armpits). And they wagged their tails anyway.

What to do. *What to do?*

There was always Plan B.

I scanned the room for Les Malt. She was an elegant older woman in silver high-heels and a silver-plum sheath dress that picked up the highlights in her hair. When I say older, I meant fiftyish to my thirtyish. She was definitely younger than my mother. Although she was all dolled up, I recognized her from her internet pictures.

I was about to approach her when Sarah, my assistant, stepped up beside me. The Christmas carolers had moved to the far end of the room so we could hear ourselves talk.

"Mr. Hancock says if you try to change the date of the presentation by using your dog to manipulate the client, you can pack your things."

So, he was watching me. And he was using

Sarah as my watchdog.

Again, I wondered. How did he even know who Sarah was? He was responsible for thousands of employees. Why out of all of those people did he know her?

I scowled and searched the floor. Wherever he was, it wasn't obvious. I made a swift sweep for Joel. He seemed to have disappeared.

"Did you hear me, boss?"

I dragged myself back from my reverie and nodded.

"Where is he?"

"Who? Hancock? He's there. By the bar. He's talking to that gorgeous woman in the gold dress."

Another one of our clients.

He was giving the woman an inordinate amount of attention. She was young, and by that I meant younger than him. She was probably mid fortyish but her looks were the type that held up. High cheekbones, large eyes and brilliantly crimson Marilyn Monroe lips. She had an outgoing personality to match. And to top it off, those stilettoes and her deep chestnut hair rolled into a stylish chignon made her taller than him.

Where were the Christmas carolers when you needed them? They were there just as you were about to have an important conversation with a person of significance, but when you needed them for a distraction, where were they?

She practically screamed confidence. What

would Natalia think of this? He was laughing at everything the woman in gold said, and attending to her every whim by keeping her glass full and the hors d'oeuvre platter at hand. So out of character for him. She was drinking pink champagne and nibbling crab puffs.

But his wife wasn't here. So how could she mind.

I stared at Mr. Hancock, hoping he could feel my disapproval. His eyes never wavered from the gorgeous woman's face. I could have started a juggling act with the pinecones from one of the tables, and he would probably have been oblivious. Apparently, as far as he was concerned, I had been dealt with.

So, if I tried to change the date of the presentation by using my dog to manipulate Les Malt, I could pack my things?

The message couldn't be any clearer than that. He could at least have had the decency to say it to my face. But of course, he would not. Not in front of his stepson. He had sent my assistant to do his dirty work for him.

Sarah's eyes returned from the bar to me.

"Who is that hunk that was with Mr. Hancock earlier?" she asked.

"That was his stepson, Joel Joseph."

"*That* was his stepson? Wow. He is gorgeous."

I suppose some people might describe him that way. I guess that meant my brother was too. I almost laughed. It was hard to think of Jonny as being gorgeous. But I had almost mistaken him for Jonny when we met him on the street.

"I wonder if he's single?"

Honestly, I did not know. And at the moment was not interested if he had a significant other. My only concern at the moment was Mr. Hancock's unreasonable attitude.

"Why is he so stubborn about this?" I whined.

Sarah crouched to pat Tang on the head. I had to hold him back so that he wouldn't ruin her scarlet party dress or the black sheer stockings beneath the mid-thigh length hem.

She glanced up at me and her sandy-colored ringlets (done specially for the party) wobbled. "You mean Hancock? I've only met him a few times, but seems to me, once he's made up his mind about something he won't change it. It makes him look weak."

It wouldn't make him look weak; it would give him a heart. And make him admirable. Compassionate.

But then some people thought compassion was weakness.

"Let me get you a drink," Sarah said, noting my despair, and went to the bar.

How I wished I had known that Joel Joseph and Magnus Hancock were related. Maybe I would have confided more to Joel when he told me he was a veterinary surgeon. But we were recent acquaintances, and the fact that he had even bothered to reassure me that there was promising treatment for Tang had left me grateful and speechless.

I didn't even know where he lived for heaven's sake. It never came up. He had to leave, and was just being polite. I would have asked him more questions except that he was already late getting back to the conference. And I had stolen enough of his time. Had I known, I would have asked him to help me with his stepfather.

The Christmas carolers sneaked up behind me and busted out into a chorus of *Baby, It's Cold Outside!*

CHAPTER 6

Since recruiting Joel's help was not an option, I approached Les Malt instead.

I waited for a break in the Christmas caroling.

"Hello, Ms. Malt," I said with forced gaiety as the carolers moved on. I'm sure she would not notice how fake my upbeat disposition was. At these social functions everyone was artificially cheerful.

She returned my greeting with a hearty handshake. I saw her nails were painted a glossy plum to complement her silver-plum dress as her thumb and first two fingers pinched the stem of a champagne flute.

"I'm Marilee Christian, one of National Pet's sales execs."

"Happy to meet you," she said. "I am looking forward to your presentation in a day or so."

I glanced down at Tang who was circling our ankles and thumping his tail against our legs. "I am so sorry, Ms. Malt."

"Please, call me Les. Everyone does."

"Les, then. Let me apologize for the exuberance of my dog."

She gently nudged him away. "He *is* a little clown, isn't he?"

I wasn't sure how to take that. But I decided to take it lightly, and as a compliment. "He just loves people."

"I can see that."

I must tread carefully. This was the CPO of the top pet store chain in the country. I mustn't lose the account. I just needed her to agree to postpone the meeting until my return.

"We love your pet store," I said. "It's Tang's favorite place to go shopping."

"Well, isn't that sweet," she said. "Be sure to ask for free samples next time you're in. Just mention my name."

I thanked her. I wished she was more of a pet lover than she seemed. She had hardly paid Tang any notice. Maybe it was because she was all dressed up in that silk dress and didn't want Tang to damage it.

"Do you have pets of your own?" I asked. Because of course she must. She owned a successful pet store chain.

"If you mean a dog or a cat, no," she said.

What else could I mean? Well, I suppose she could have a bird or fish or some other small animal… but she wasn't elaborating. And just from appearances and speaking with her for a few moments, I highly doubted it.

"With my busy career it wouldn't be fair to have a dog waiting hours for me to come home. And there is all the travelling I do for my job as well. Sometimes I think I'm away more often than I am at home." She gave an artificial sigh of distress and lowered her lashes. "I wish I could, but I have no time for a dog."

"So, you're a dog person," I said hopefully.

"I'm not partial to either. All pets are equal in my books." She gave me a knowing smile.

She would have to say that. If she showed any bias people would stop shopping at her stores. Oh, crap. How to do this. Should I just tell her about Tang and assume she would sympathize?

"Les," I said. "I hope I'm not being too presumptuous. Although I'm eager to meet with you and your team day after tomorrow, I—"

"Ms. Christian!" Magnus Hancock's voice boomed out of the dim lighting behind me.

I swung around to see my boss, face prune-colored in the dark light. I'm sure Les Malt would have notice nothing. I, on the other hand, could feel his rage.

He was gripping a glass of Scotch, and the ice in it tinkled as he greeted the Chief Purchasing Officer of the EveryPet Emporium. His over exuberance was an attempt to mask his true feelings. Which had nothing to do with Les Malt, and everything to do with me. "We are so looking forward to impressing you and your team with Ms. Christian's presentation. She's a powerhouse that one. You won't be able to resist!"

He finished his drink and handed the glass to a passing server dressed in black, red and white. And accepted another. "Care for another drink?" he asked Les Malt.

She shook her head and indicated the half-drunk flute of champagne in her right hand. He sent the server on his way without offering me a drink, then made further chitchat with the CPO, all the while forcibly including me in the conversation for an appropriate and polite amount of time before he excused us. "Look forward to meeting the team," Hancock said, shaking Les Malt's hand vigorously.

"Likewise," she said. "I'm already impressed. Love your dress by the way." This comment was directed at me.

My vintage velvet was unique. No one else wore anything like it.

"Thank you," I said.

"Be prepared to be wowed by this one." Hancock indicated me and I forced a smile. "Smart and stylish."

"Ms. Malt," I said, taking the opportunity to cut in, since they were discussing my merits. "Would it be too much to ask if we could reschedule?"

Before Les Malt could answer Mr. Hancock

interrupted. "She's kidding. A big kidder, this one. We'll see you Tuesday."

He turned on the charm, then told her to enjoy the party while he attended to the other guests.

What he did in fact was drag me off to a quiet corner, Tang in tow, to browbeat me.

"What were you trying to pull, Marilee. Did you not hear my orders?"

Orders?

"I told you not to attempt to change the date."

"I didn't." He hadn't given me the chance to. He had cut me off before Les Malt could consider my request.

"You could lose this account if you do."

A sharp pause on my part. "How do you know that?"

"Are you questioning me?"

"No, Mr. Hancock."

"Now, go home before you cause any trouble."

Shock made me speechless. Honestly, there was no comprehending his behavior. But the tension between us was so thick I could barely breathe. Time to admit defeat. I turned to go. Then out of the corner of my eye I caught him glaring.

Why was he so angry? What harm could it do? Admittedly, I did not know my boss well, but this was uncharacteristic behavior even for him.

I tugged on Tang's leash and he pranced my way.

I turned back. Hancock was waiting for me

to leave before he returned to his guests. But I suddenly realized I wasn't finished with this topic yet.

How could he possibly know that changing the date of the presentation would be a problem? I saw him tense. Had he read my mind? Or maybe my body language. And that only strengthened my determination.

"Look Mr. Hancock. I've done well for this company, haven't I?"

He said nothing. No contradiction there.

"How could it hurt to hear her response?"

The look of exasperation on his face was all the answer I needed.

Still, I was not deterred. "She didn't appear upset when I asked her the first time. I'm going to ask her again."

"If you do, Marilee. You are fired."

I opened my mouth to object but I could see I had no case. He was never going to see my side of things. What's more, I had a feeling this decision had more to do with him than it had to do with me.

And it had nothing at all to do with Tang.

I closed my mouth. It was so unfair. So irrational. Nevertheless, I took him at his word, bade him goodnight and started for the exit.

That scene with him preyed on my mind. What

was going on here? Why was he so inflexible? And why was he drinking so much? He positively reeked of whiskey. It was just as likely the client would be put off by an inebriated CEO. And if it really was Les Malt who was the issue, why would my asking her to reschedule be so problematic?

I was about to go back and ask him, when Sarah returned with my drink. I had forgotten all about it. What had taken her so long? Then it occurred to me that she had probably seen me preoccupied by the boss and the CPO of EveryPet.

The cocktail was a bright pink Cosmo with a pale green, paper umbrella jabbed into a wedge of lime.

"Thanks, Sarah," I said, accepting the drink then placing it down on a nearby table. "But I won't be staying."

"You have to stay," she insisted. "The party has only just started."

Tang was dancing at her feet and she bent down to give him a dog cookie. "I brought you something, too." The treat was one of National Pet's latest peanut butter creations, shaped like a squirrel.

He raised his paw. Then the other paw. I had taught him to shake paws for treats, and now it was second nature. Sarah laughed and popped it into his mouth. He wolfed it down. Was that going to be the last cookie he could ever eat? The vet hadn't elaborated much on the nature of his recovery after the surgery.

But tonight, he was enjoying himself and I wasn't about to spoil it.

Sarah rose. "I heard what Hancock said." Her voice was low to avoid being overheard. That wasn't a problem as there was enough noise to make normal speech unintelligible.

I wished I didn't sound so whiny. "I just don't understand why he's so certain that my asking to push the date forward is an issue."

"I think I might know," Sarah said.

My eyebrows hiked in surprise. Although I guess I should have expected it. Sarah was one of those people that seemed to know everything that was going on. I only knew about things if someone informed me directly. Sarah seemed to be a magnet that sucked up gossip.

"What is it?" I demanded.

Sarah hesitated. Something was going on inside that creative brain of hers and I could only guess. She dragged me to a quieter corner where no people were mingling. The Christmas lights left only shadows on this part of the room. We were by the wall behind two grand, white pillars, practically hidden from sight. Even so, she glanced furtively around the room like some sort of industrial spy. No one was taking any particular notice of us. Why should they? This was a party. People were getting drunk and having fun. Why she bothered to lower her voice to a whisper is beyond me, but what she finally divulged threw me for a loop.

"I don't know if this is true exactly, but apparently, Les Malt is a horse lover."

I was stumped to speechlessness. What did that have to do with anything? Especially, what did it have to do with changing the date of my presentation?

"Apparently, her horse is lame. She's had this horse forever."

So that was what Les Malt had meant when I'd asked her if she had a pet. No, she had no pet if I meant a dog or a cat. Were horses considered pets? I was beginning to realize that maybe horses were in a class of their own.

"She has scheduled the vet to come to put the horse down the day after the presentation."

Oh, dear lord. No wonder Mr. Hancock didn't want me to push the date forward or back. Either way would be upsetting.

Why couldn't he have told me that?

Because I was an employee. Not a friend. And certainly not family. This was the personal affairs of a client and not my business.

And yet, since Ms. Malt and I were both kind of going through the same thing…? I ran my palms up and down over the smooth velvet skirt of my dress.

No. I had no idea how she would react.

Although I knew exactly Mr. Hancock's stand on the situation.

That left me only one choice.

"Thanks, for telling me, Sarah. But do me a

favor and keep this information to yourself. I'm not going to ask you how you acquired it, but I think it's best not to spread gossip. If Mr. Hancock didn't see fit to tell me, then it's because he didn't want me to know."

She looked a little affronted as though I had just accused her of rumormongering. Well, I guess I had. However, gossiping was never a good idea. Entertaining yourself and your peers at the expense of others could backfire.

"I just meant that this is very personal to Ms. Malt. And I believe Mr. Hancock was trying to respect that."

"Sure," she said. "I was only trying to help."

She barely said goodbye as I took my leave with a grateful smile. On her face was a look of annoyance, or was it disgust? Had I offended her? I hadn't meant to. She had just done me a good turn which I thoroughly appreciated. I only meant that rumormongering could lead to negative effects like misunderstandings and hurt feelings. And an invasion of privacy.

I decided not to analyze it and walked out the door.

CHAPTER 7

I missed work the following day. I called Sarah just before leaving for the airport to apologize if I had offended her by insinuating that she was a gossip.

Her gossip was very helpful, and had prevented me from a deep dive into a big fat *faux pas*. I told her the ball was in her court. All of my materials were on my computer, including the PowerPoint. She was prepared to take over. I thanked her again for preventing me from making a huge mistake.

She was gracious and quite optimistic.

"If you land this account," I said. "You will probably inherit my job." I had already resigned myself to this very inevitable possibility. "Blow them away, Sarah," I said. "And good luck."

I shoved my phone inside my purse and had a last look around. It was not like I would be gone for very long. But I had a strange feeling my life was about to change. I loved this townhouse. It was located right on the waterfront in False Creek. It had two bedrooms, one of which opened out to a tiled courtyard with a marvelous view of the marina, a large marble bathroom, an ultra-modern kitchen, dining and living area that also opened out to a flagstone patio, and a study where I kept all my murder mysteries.

Outside, the light was thin, the air cold. It was just after dawn and the taxi was already waiting to take us to the airport.

Tang was in his little carrier as we waited in line to board the plane. Last month I was awarded a bonus for landing a new client. It may be reckless of me since I may very well be out of my six-figure job (in fact, I was practically certain of it) but I meant to spend a portion of it on a Business Class ticket. Unfortunately, it was not to be. Booking at such short notice meant most of the desirable seats were gone. And since Air Canada had a sale on Business Class, all of the seats had been snapped up.

Could things get any worse?

Yes, they could.

We were stuck in Coach, in the middle of the plane, with two screaming children on the window side of me. Oh no. Much as I loved my own niece and nephew—Michael and Mia—other people's kids could mean a fright show. But I had experience (God knows how many hours I had spent babysitting them) and had learned patience, so I could weather it out. Besides when I thought about it even sweet Michael and Mia had their sibling squabbles. This one with the two boys was only marginally more spirited.

Good thing, I was in the aisle seat. At least I could turn my back on them if they got too enthusiastic.

I managed to shove Tang's carrier under the seat in front of me, with the hopes that later in the flight I could remove him from confinement. The flight attendant had promised that I could.

But for takeoff, we had to be fastened down.

The children's mother was sitting behind us in the middle seat and was kicking up a fuss about not being able to sit with her boys. Yes, my flight companions were two boys, somewhere in the neighborhood of ten and eleven years old.

The airline attendant approached me sheepishly. She was tall, of medium weight and build, and had the kind of face and voice that made you feel comfortable. Not classically pretty, but attractive nonetheless. She was mid-fortyish with her recent gray and natural blond blending stylishly in a mid-length herringbone bob. Loved those white, gray, copper and chestnut streaks.

She smoothed down the skirt of her uniform and said, "I'm sorry to bother you, but the woman behind would like to sit with her sons."

The squabbling beside me escalated. I had no doubt as to whom she referred. "Would you mind trading seats with her?"

That would mean Tang would be squashed under a middle seat. And me? They had no idea how this might affect my aerophobia.

Being more than slightly claustrophobic, I needed to be on the aisle. Otherwise, uncontrollable panic set in. That was why I always flew Business Class. For the extra space. And in that, my company had always been accommodating. This time, however, I was paying for the flight.

"Those boys beside you," she elaborated. My silence had her confused, as though I had misunderstood the request.

I knew exactly who she meant, and what she was asking. I shook my head. "I'm sorry."

I explained the situation in as few words as possible, and when the flight attendant realized I was travelling with a small, sick dog, and we were on our way across the country so that he could obtain a life-saving procedure, she apologized.

And that was enough to convince her that both parties had good reasons for wanting their demands met.

However, only one of us could be accommodated, and since I had paid for this aisle seat—probably having beat the other woman out on it by seconds when I purchased it online—I had no choice but to insist.

The flight attendant explained to the complainant that it was not possible. When politely asked, the passengers on either side of her were unwilling to give up their seats too. Because like me, they had paid for specific seats. In this case, window and aisle seats, and had their own reasons for choosing them.

Harassed, the flight attendant left to deal with other passengers, and we were all left feeling tense and upset.

The woman behind me was more than just upset. When I half-rose to explain my situation to her directly—the fact that I had to sedate myself before I could even get on a plane—she spat, "That's just an excuse for being selfish."

I was selfish?

I couldn't take any more of this. My heart was ricocheting against my ribcage, and my breath was short. My fingers tingled and the airplane cabin was beginning to swim. I understood why she wanted to sit with her sons. But they seemed to be fine on their own. If I was willing to put up with their racket, why couldn't she just let it be?

She was livid; her face matched the color of her wrinkled blouse. The blouse failed to enhance any good features she might have had; her personality was that overbearing. And FYI her hair was bright blue, tied in a high ponytail, clashing against the red blouse. A peculiar fashion choice considering what she was wearing, but if it was attention she was craving, this would do it. Even without the screaming boys.

"They shouldn't even allow dogs in the cabin," she snapped. "Filthy, smelly things."

Okay. This woman could not be reasoned with. I turned and sat down.

I was tempted to take another Xanax to calm me down. But should I risk being unconscious when we landed?

As the squabbling continued, I grit my teeth. This was going to be a long flight.

The blue-haired woman wasn't finished yet. She suddenly slapped the back of my headrest, forcing me to jerk upright and twist to look between the seats. Out of my peripheral vision I glimpsed the crinkly red top and black tights rise. Her lurid face appeared over the top of the headrest. The vision was cartoonish and if it wasn't such a serious situation I might have laughed. She raised a fist. Was she going to assault me? And demanded that I give up my seat?

"You aren't sitting with anyone," she insisted angrily. "Where is your consideration? Do you really want to spend the next five hours putting up with that?"

She threw a thick, baseball-bat-shaped forearm over my head at the window where her boys were vigorously stabbing each other with straws and giggling. When the arm returned, I thought she was going to hit me.

The flight attendant was returning, heels tapping with determined deliberation. The disturbance was upsetting other passengers and someone must have buzzed for service.

Was she going to force me to switch seats? I almost felt like doing it. Then the flight crew would have to, not only deal with the unruly family of three, but also with me climbing over my neighbor passenger, gasping for air in the grips of a full-blown panic attack, and screeching down the aisle clawing for a way out of this flying tin can at an altitude of 30,000 feet.

Get a grip. Calm down.

I glanced below to see that Tang was lying comfortably, oblivious of my distress. The Xanax I had taken to calm my nerves prior to flight time had ceased to work.

"Ms. Christian?" the flight attendant said.

I glanced up, ready to dig my boots in, and barely able to breathe.

"My name is Hazel. Would you mind coming with me? We've found quieter seating elsewhere, that you might enjoy. It is also on the aisle."

What else could I do? This craziness could not continue. I agreed and reached below to feel for Tang's carrier.

The flight attendant nodded over my headrest at the red-faced, blue-haired woman who had finally stopped berating me.

Hazel didn't bother addressing the woman by name. By now everyone in Coach knew who she was because of all the ruckus and because she had frozen in mid stand with a self-satisfied smirk on her face when she realized she had gotten her way.

"You can sit with your children," Hazel said amenably.

Hazel apologized to the man who was sitting on the aisle-side of the red bloused, blue-ponytailed woman. "Do you mind?"

He happily rose so that the woman could reach the aisle.

Meanwhile, I pulled Tang's carrier out of the slot beneath the seat in front of me and popped it on my lap before handing it to the flight attendant, who accepted it with appropriate care, as there was a live pet inside it.

"Any other carryon?" she asked as I made my way out.

I shook my head. Lugging Tang and my purse was enough.

"Good." She smiled, swinging her gorgeous bobbed herringbone do. "Come this way please."

Instead of moving to the rear of the plane we were making our way to the front. Wherever this seat was, it had to be better than what I had just left. As long as it was on the aisle. My nerves were shot and I was ready to go ballistic. It took every grain of self-control I had to keep from strangling that woman. Please, *please* take me to a nice quiet aisle seat!

She had promised that it was.

"We've had a no-show in Business Class," Hazel

said and drew apart the barrier. "You've been upgraded, and are welcome to sit here."

I gaped in relief and sheer pleasure. The air even smelled fresher here. And spacious. The seats were so spacious, each semi private, angled with partitions, and there was even a ventilated kennel to put my dog.

"After take-off," she said. "You can place your pup on your lap. Just don't let him wander around the rest of the plane."

"I can't thank you enough," I said.

She winked at me. "The pleasure is all mine."

I tucked Tang in his carrier inside the ventilated kennel and latched the door. Once secure, I took to my comfortable seat and fastened my seatbelt. I ran my fingers over the fine textured fabric, sighing with relief. Talk about a lucky break. Had Hazel not found me this seat I would have lost it.

Breathe, breathe, breathe. Why did flying always make me feel like screaming? Apparently, forty percent of the population had anxiety over flying. One in five of those people needed alcohol or prescription drugs to get through the flight. I was not alone.

The In-flight Service Supervisor was making an announcement. We were about to take off. Everyone was required to return to their seats and buckle up.

Hazel returned to the crew's station. I checked Tang once more and then secured my seatbelt.

The engines roared to life. I held my breath. The plane raced down the runway, my heart racing in unison. My stomach lurched and my ears plugged, then popped. We were airborne.

Poor Tang. I couldn't imagine what he was feeling.

"Good morning passengers. This is your captain speaking. Welcome to Air Canada Flight 877. We are currently cruising at an altitude of 33,000 feet at an airspeed of 400 mph. The time is 8:15 am Vancouver time. The weather is fair with a tailwind on our side. We are expecting to arrive at our destination of Toronto approximately twenty minutes early. Currently, the city of Toronto is overcast and rainy. But we are expecting things to clear by our arrival... In a few minutes, the cabin crew will be coming around to offer you snacks and beverages. I will talk to you again before we reach our destination. Until then, sit back, relax and enjoy the flight."

After the captain's announcement, I reached down to release Tang from the kennel.

He looked slightly bewildered but not particularly stressed. The first thing he did when I hauled him onto my lap was wag his tail and give me a happy bark.

I shushed him, although I was pretty sure the

hum of the engine pretty much drowned out his song of joy.

Inside my oversized purse was Tang's winter sweater, and I removed it, letting it unroll as I drew it out. The air conditioning was a little cool and I didn't want him to get cold. The sweater was tube-like with two holes for his front limbs. And slid on the same way you would pull a sweater over a child's head. A little long for his body, I had to fold up the hem like a tuque. It was handmade by my sister-in-law who didn't know the first thing about dog clothes. But it was the thought and the loving effort that counted. And it had become my and Tang's favorite item of clothing. If it could be said that Tang had a favorite. Like most dogs he preferred his birthday suit.

His back was to me and I stroked a hand down his spine. He had lost a little weight and that had me concerned. He however was quite content and turned to face me, and I planted a firm one on his forehead. This was his first flight. And he sincerely appeared to be enjoying it.

I glanced to the adjacent window, next to another semi-private seat which currently was empty so I could see the view outside. We were cruising above the clouds and the sun and sky were clear and bright with a slight wintery hue. *This isn't so bad,* I told myself as I picked up the royal blue dog sweater.

I looked down at Tang. And he looked up with

shiny, gleeful eyes. Tang certainly thought so and assured me vocally.

I was just about to roll the handknit sweater over his head when a voice spoke from behind us. I jolted upright in my seat when I saw who it was.

"Thought I recognized that happy bark."

Joel, dressed in a moss green, form-fitting pullover stood at the entrance to my partitioned seat grinning at me. "Looks like we're going to be fellow passengers."

"Joel! How nice to see you. What are you doing here?"

"Heading home," he said. "Conference ended yesterday."

I was genuinely surprised and pleased to see him. Something in the vicinity of my heart gave a leap. Joy or acid reflux. Or both? "Hope it was productive," I said.

"It was. Always learn something new. Here, let me help you with that." He reached out to take the sweater that was hanging from one hand.

"Where are you sitting?" I asked.

He pointed to the other side of me at the empty seat.

"Why, we're practically neighbors!"

Tang stumbled off my lap and Joel caught him, legs akimbo. I picked up the sweater that Joel had dropped on my lap.

Joel held Tang out away from his body so that I could put his sweater on. Tang wasn't having any of it, and struggled until Joel hauled him back against his chest. There he went limp.

"Hello little dude. What a cute sweater. Did your mommy make it?"

I giggled. Yes, it was obviously homemade, but it was my brother's wife Eva who was the artisan, not me.

"Looks like it was made exactly for him."

"It was," I said. "Though Eva knows very little about canine anatomy. As you can see, she knitted it as though it were meant for a little human." I poked my fingers through the sleeve holes.

He chuckled. "It's adorable." Then he returned to Tang. "How are you liking your airplane ride, little guy? And my goodness. You're travelling Business Class. You lucky dog!"

"Yes, we *were* kind of lucky," I agreed and proceeded to tell him the whole laughable tale concerning the irate mother with the blue hair and her high-strung boys.

His smile was really something. "So, all's well that ends well. To use a cliché."

"So far," I said and crossed my fingers.

CHAPTER 8

"So, you live in Ontario?" I asked.

"Yes," he replied. "Born and bred there."

"My mother lives in Toronto. I usually come out once a year to visit. And every other Christmas. But as you know… this is an unscheduled event." I glanced over at Tang who was comfortably limp in Joel's arms.

Shih Tzus for some reason become quite passive when held. I think it has something to do with their history of being emperors' dogs. They were bred to be social companions, especially to serve as lapdogs, and were pretty much useless for anything else. Try training a Shih Tzu to fetch. They'll catch the ball or toy—well, catch probably isn't the right word, more like chase—but they won't bring it back. They're just as likely to lie comfortably with the toy and chew on it. Or use it for a pillow.

This was the preferred behavior in the royal

household.

"They caught the tumor early," Joel reminded me. "The prognosis is good. Try not to worry. Everything that can be done, will be done for him... Hey, sorry I wasn't able to chat longer with you at the party. Magnus wanted to introduce me to a bunch of his clients. Then when I finally broke away and looked around for you, you were gone."

He handed Tang back to me and I sat him on my lap. I still found it hard to believe that Joel was related by marriage to my boss.

"Something wrong?" Joel asked, noticing my frown.

I glanced up at him, then looked down at Tang and began rolling his sweater over his head. "I went home early. I didn't much feel like partying." I paused from fiddling with his ears. Then decided it wouldn't hurt if I told Joel about Les Malt and my failed plan to change my presentation date because of Sarah's gossip.

Joel was stunned by the story. I was stunned that he was stunned. I looked up from threading Tang's right paw through the sweater's sleeve hole. Tang dropped his paw as my grip on it slackened.

"You mean Sarah Phipps?" he asked. "*She* told you that story?"

Okay, now I was even more stunned. "You *know* Sarah?"

"I met her at the Christmas party. She seemed like a nice woman. We ended up spending some time together. Turns out we both did our undergrad at U of T. Although we weren't there at the same time, considering I'm twelve years older than her."

They went to the same university? My mind spun backwards in time to the day I interviewed Sarah for the position of my assistant. For the life of me I was certain that her CV said she got a B.A. from the University of British Columbia. Not the University of Toronto. Could I be mistaken? I finished putting Tang's other paw through the hole and straightened the sweater over his back.

"Asked me out for coffee," he added.

My eyes widened. That girl moved fast. When she saw what she wanted, she went for it. I could learn a thing or two from her.

"Did you go?" Not that it was any of my business.

"I did."

"Oh."

He was studying my face, puzzled by my reaction. Was he wondering if I minded? I had no right to mind. He and I weren't dating; we weren't even friends really. We were what? Acquaintances at best.

I was trying not to stare, forcing myself to not even look. I busied myself by folding the hem of Tang's sweater up an inch.

If he liked Sarah, what could I do about it? She was young, attractive, personable, super outgoing and intelligent. Why wouldn't he like her? She had the guts to ask him out. The thought had not even occurred to me.

The next thing he said blew me away.

"Les Malt doesn't have a horse."

My eyes flashed wide. What? How would he know?

He smiled that fabulous smile again. "She's my mother's best friend. I would know if she had a horse."

My frown deepened as the episode at the Christmas party with Sarah replayed in my mind. She had fabricated the whole thing? How bizarre.

"Why would Sarah lie?" I mused aloud.

He shrugged. I really hadn't meant the question to be heard. Joel was already gone when she told me that story about Les Malt's horse.

Reality suddenly sank in.

There was no beloved injured horse that needed to be euthanized!

Then it dawned on me. Sarah had spun me that yarn because she knew if I couldn't move the date of the presentation, I would have no choice but to miss it.

How manipulative! I would never have guessed. As my assistant, Sarah had always been accommodating, cooperative and helpful. And all the while she actually had a deceitful, conniving brain. I had always known she was ambitious, and no stranger to gossip, but I would never have guessed that she would stoop so low as to invent a story to give her an advantage. If it wasn't so distasteful and had I not been the victim, I would say she was just plain smart.

Now I understood. She would get the chance to impress the big client if I was gone.

And ultimately—get my job.

Mr. Hancock was totally wrong about her. She would be perfect for the job.

My head collapsed in my hands. What an idiot I was.

But either way. It made no difference. I could hardly turn back now. Even if I wanted to. We were in midflight. I still had to go against my boss's wishes. For Tang's sake.

I glanced hopelessly at Joel. I was back to square one. With no reasonable explanation for why Mr. Hancock refused to move the date of the presentation and why he forbade me to ask Les Malt to consider it. If only I had persisted. Maybe she would have sympathized and changed the date.

No point in bemoaning my lack of backbone now.

I wanted desperately to ask Joel about Hancock. The man was being unreasonably stubborn. Was something going on that I was ignorant of?

Joel's concern was obvious in the tone of his voice. "Something I said upset you."

I should be better than that. All my training in sales had taught me to hide my emotions.

My emotions were irrelevant if I wished to be successful. The people's emotions that mattered were the buyers. Clue into those and you had them where you wanted them. This was the golden rule of marketing.

"Marilee… Mari, did I say something wrong?"

I was stunned by his perceptiveness. Or maybe my face had betrayed me and was revealing all of my feelings. I thought I'd gotten that under control when I became an executive sales rep. I guess not.

Could I trust him? Would I be stepping over the line if I asked if his stepfather was suffering some personal crisis? Or was Hancock always so unreasonable? Or was it just me?

Maybe it was something personal. A health issue? Why was he drinking so much? Or was the company in trouble? I know Hancock mentioned something about repercussions and layoffs if I didn't land the account with EveryPet. Oh dear. Had I really left my boss in the lurch?

Generosity was not always my best trait, but this time I had to try harder. It was probably over for me, but I prayed that Sarah would wow them. For her sake as well as to appease my own conscience. It was too late for me to be angry with her for manipulating me out of the game. I would have gone against Mr. Hancock's wishes anyway.

Did I not say she was smart?

Joel gazed at me, waiting for a reply. At first glance, Joel did look remarkably like my brother.

But now that I had seen him a few times I realized he looked a lot less like him than I had originally thought. The main similarities were in their height and build. They were both tall and fit. But their coloring and hairstyles were similar too. As was the stubbly beard. And their personalities. Both kind; both good. But when you looked at their faces, you could see they were hardly twins. Plus, Joel was a couple years younger.

They say that women often chose men that reminded them of their fathers. Was that true of brothers as well? My dad was no longer in my life.

I was going off-track. How could I be sizing him up as a potential romantic interest when my life was falling apart? When I failed to show up at the meeting, that would be the end of the line for me. The time on my phone where it sat on the console read 9:05am. Even as we spoke, Sarah was stealing my job.

And then there was Tang.

Asking Joel if he knew of any problems my boss was having might be a bad idea. Joel and I were barely acquainted. And if Mr. Hancock had seen it as inappropriate to let me know the details of what troubled him, how could I ask his stepson?

"Was it something I said or did at the party?" Joel asked. I had waited too long to reply and now he was trying to second guess me.

I must set the record straight. But not too straight. Was the truth appropriate here? How did you pry into someone's life without prying?

"I had this trip to get ready for," I said. It was better than saying nothing. He had been so considerate and thoughtful I had to allay the tension. "It was hard for me to enjoy the party. I was too distracted so I thought it best to go home early," I finished lamely. That much was the absolute truth.

Joel nodded sympathetically. "I understand your concern. But Tang will have the very best care at the OVC. I can tell you, firsthand, it's the best facility there is in Canada. I trained there myself."

Really? Oh, if only he was still there. It dawned on me that I had failed to catch the name of the surgeon who would be operating on my dog. I would feel so much better knowing the surgeon handling Tang's case was Joel.

I said, "You have a practice in Toronto?"

He nodded. Apparently, he had his own clinic on a nice street in the core of the city in the colorful, gentrified neighborhood of Cabbage Town. He lived in a restored Victorian home in that same neighborhood. And he wasn't kidding when he said he had no wife or kids. Just two golden retrievers and a Persian cat. Who currently were under the care of a neighbor. No mention of a girlfriend. But that didn't mean he wasn't dating.

"I specialize in dogs and cats but I've treated the occasional ferret, Macaw, guinea pig and bunny rabbit." He smiled and changed the subject. "So, what do you do at National Pet?"

"Oh, I'm in sales. I go after the big clients. Though, I'm pretty sure I won't have a job to go back to after this."

My hand flew to my mouth. I hadn't meant to blurt that out. There was no guarantee he would be on my side so I mustn't badmouth his stepdad.

He looked puzzled. "Magnus fired you?" He glanced at Tang. "Whatever for?"

Joel must have had a good idea why his stepfather had fired me. But clearly, he did not want to jump to conclusions.

"Look Joel. I don't want to drag you into this. What's done is done."

His frown deepened. "What did you do?"

My pride was garbage; I let it spill. "I went against your stepfather's wishes. He told me not to go to Guelph today. I have an important pitch to make tomorrow for the company. And yet here I am."

My reasons were self-explanatory and I decided to leave out the details.

"He made you choose between your dog and your job?"

Well, now *that* made him sound like the evil King Herod who had killed off all of Bethlehem's firstborn sons. Simply to ensure his own self-interests. It wasn't exactly like that. And I explained the options Mr. Hancock had suggested.

"He's right." I sighed. "I'm not the best person

for the job."

"No one should be asked to make that kind of choice."

I couldn't allow him to believe that his stepfather was a heartless monster. Although I know what I would have done if I were in his place. But I was me and he wasn't. He had an important corporation to run. And I didn't. Sometimes things hung on one single meeting. I knew my job and how to do it. I knew next to nothing about running a large business. I only knew that I loved my dog.

"He wasn't asking me to choose my job over my dog, Joel. He was just asking me to send someone else with Tang until after the presentation. But I had no one who could go on such short notice. No one I could trust. And besides..." The lump in my throat was huge, and the ache in my heart unbearable. "I couldn't not go; he's my baby Tang," I ended in a whisper.

A tear fell on Tang's head and he raised his head and licked my wet chin.

"I'm sorry, bambino. Mummy's okay." I cuddled him like it might be for the last time.

Oh, why didn't Joel just leave so I could blubber in private. I wiped my cheek with my shoulder, still holding Tang to my chest.

"I'll talk to Magnus," Joel said. "I'm sure he was over-reacting. It isn't like him to be so unsympathetic."

My voice managed to come out without

croaking. "He runs a multinational corporation. He can't afford to sympathize with one employee and her dog."

His brow creased in thought. "Still…" He looked up. "I think I'll give him a call. See what's up."

I saw how Mr. Hancock had seen right through me, guessing my plan before I was able to execute it. I couldn't use his stepson that way. It was wrong. "I can't let you do that."

Besides I had already gone against his wishes. I wasn't exactly standing at the front of the boardroom with a laser pointer practicing my pitch for why National Pet should be showcased at every single EveryPet franchise.

He was never going to hire me back if he thought I had manipulated his stepson into aiding and abetting me.

CHAPTER 9

"Thank you so much, Hazel" I said to the flight attendant who had rescued me and Tang from experiencing the flight from Hell.

She was replete in full dress uniform, a Sloane-style black dress with red belt and scarf, and a black blazer. She smiled as we stood at the exit ready to debark at the Pearson International Airport. Despite the difficult circumstances the flight had turned out to be a memorable experience.

"You've been so wonderful." I felt like hugging her, but with all the other passengers waiting to disembark I decided to refrain. They might think I had gotten special treatment. Which I had.

"You are welcome," she said, pleasantly. "Delighted to be able to help. So glad you enjoyed your flight. And maybe we'll see you again. On your return flight?"

I was meeting with the vet before the surgery.

Tang's operation was scheduled for tomorrow morning. With luck and if the procedure went well, we could be headed for home by week's end.

"That would be the best-case scenario."

Tang was inside the carrier and I held the handle tight in my right hand. Hazel bent her head to look inside and air-kissed Tang goodbye. His handknit royal blue sweater had been a hit with the flight crew too. "Hope to see you again, little guy."

His response was an enthusiastic thumping of his tail against the polyester walls.

I waved goodbye and Joel followed behind us.

"Don't worry about anything, Mari," he said.

Despite my mood I was pleased that he was calling me Mari instead of Marilee. That was what my friends and family called me. Did that mean we were friends? "That's like asking a dog to stop eating."

Joel chuckled. "Don't worry about that either. He'll be eating like a hog in a few days after the procedure."

I guess he would know. My smile was genuine. At that moment I believed him.

"I'll get to the bottom of what's going on with Magnus too."

If my gratitude got any bigger, I would explode.

We parted ways with Joel at the baggage claim area after collecting our suitcases and exchanging cellphone numbers. He had a car waiting for him and I had prebooked a taxi for the trip to Guelph.

"Don't forget. Keep me posted," he said.

"I promise." I squeezed the business card he had given me that had his cellphone number handwritten on the back.

He patted Tang on the head. I had released him from his carrier shortly after we arrived at the baggage claim. "Hey, Mari, I mean it. I know it feels impossible right now but try not to worry so much. Tang will be in excellent hands."

"Thanks, Joel. And thank you for keeping us company on the flight. It really helped take my mind off things."

"My pleasure," he said.

Joel went in the opposite direction from me to find his car in the airport parking lot. I stood watching him until he disappeared down the long corridor before glancing at his card.

I cherished his handwritten cellphone number and I cherished this card. I held it in my hand seconds longer than necessary before I slipped it inside the key compartment of my purse and zipped it tight, then I fastened the snaps on my parka and stepped outside through the sliding glass doors.

Rolling my suitcase on its wheels with the carrier stacked on top of it and Tang on his leash at my feet, I approached the Taxi rank. Cold air slapped me in the face and I braced myself against the wind. Rows of cars were accepting passengers, and I saw further along, a man leaning out of a car window. "Are you Marilee Christian?" he called.

"Yes," I shouted and hurried with my luggage. Tang in his blue sweater scrambled alongside of me and the man exited the car to help with the luggage.

"Cold night," he said and smiled at Tang's winter gear.

I agreed.

"Is that it?" he asked, stuffing the trunk.

I nodded and he slammed the lid down, and then opened the backseat door for me to get in with my dog. I was about to put Tang back inside his carrier when the cabbie said, "No. Don't do that. He's fine on your lap."

How kind of him. But my lap was not my intention. I dangled a metal and fabric contraption. "Is it okay if I attach his seatbelt back there?" I asked.

"Of course," he said.

I had hired the car to take us directly to Guelph. The destination was the Ontario Veterinary College hospital.

We were headed in the opposite direction of rush hour so the traffic was light. I had been feeling pretty positive during the flight over, largely due to the attentiveness of Hazel and Joel. Especially, because of Joel. We had spent the greater portion of the trip learning about each other and playing with Tang.

The cab driver was chatty and although I was exhausted, I tried to be polite. He noticed my reticence and turned quiet. He was considerate, and I was grateful.

As I watched the passing traffic through the side window, the light dulled to nightfall and my mood sank. It even looked to be threatening rain, if not snow. The clouds on the horizon looked bruised and grim, and the wet black road seemed to wind into eternity. There were very few trees and any grass or scrub were now dead and brown. Frozen puddles littered the highway frosted with white.

The winter landscape was bleak, as bleak as I felt. And now it was starting to snow. Flurries of it driven by the wind slammed into the windows. The *slap slap slap* of the windshield wipers could barely keep up.

The cab driver must have detected my anxiety. "Ontario winters," he said over his shoulder. "You're not from around here, are you?"

"No," I said into his rearview mirror. "We're from Vancouver."

"Ah…" A knowing nod. It seldom snowed in December on the lower mainland of the west coast. "So, what brings you out here? Visiting family for Christmas?"

It was still two weeks before Christmas but it would have been a good answer had I not been so distraught. I decided to tell him the truth and gave him the short form of the story. He was silent for a moment. Was he sorry he had asked?

"I wish it would stop blowing," I said to break

the silence.

"Don't worry, miss," the cab driver said. His voice was kind but determined. "I will get you there."

The clouds had knitted together into a thick dark mass. The last light vanished and the snow blew in earnest. I could feel the wind batting against the side of the car. A terrifying feeling, almost as bad as turbulence on a plane.

The driver turned all his concentration on the road. We were now in the midst of a blizzard. In front of us a salt truck was dumping salt onto the highway, and some of it was flying into our windshield. He squinted and swerved to avoid the worst of it.

I gripped the edge of my seat with one hand and my dog with the other. The snow fell so fast the tracks of the salt truck filled in as soon as they formed.

The cabbie plowed through the horrific storm. The wipers flapped furiously as the flakes thickened layer upon layer on the windows. We were driving practically blind.

CHAPTER 10

The storm finally lightened and the snow began to stop. Outside the hospital, several evergreens, decorated with colored lights, glowed prettily through the thick veil of white. The cheeriness conflicted with my mood. It was hard to reconcile the joy of Christmas with my current sadness.

I asked the taxi driver to wait with our luggage while we attended the appointment. I knew that was going to cost me a fortune, but I wanted to be sure I had a ride waiting.

"It won't be more than an hour," I promised, though I had no right to do that as I didn't know for sure.

"I will turn off the meter while I wait."

"No. You mustn't do that."

But because the cab driver had learned our reason for visiting Guelph, he could do no less. He was touched that we had flown all the way from

Vancouver so that Tang could be treated at the Ontario Veterinary College hospital—the very best veterinary facility in the country.

We stood at the curb where I paid him for the trip from Toronto.

"I won't hear of it," he insisted. "This little guy deserves the best." He was facing me in front of the hospital as he processed my payment on his credit card machine. He handed me the receipt and tucked the gadget onto his front console through the side door. He got down on his haunches and scratched Tang under the chin. "You are a brave soul, little *amico*," he said.

I was touched by his kindness.

"What's your name?" I asked.

"Bruno." He rose to his feet. He was about fortyish. Italian by his name and accent, and a veteran cabbie.

"My name is Marilee. But please call me Mari. Tang and I cannot thank you enough."

If only Mr. Hancock was like Bruno.

"I could not, in good conscience, charge you an hour, when I am not driving you anywhere. I will take an early dinner break and come back for you. In an hour, you say?"

I nodded. Bruno almost had me in tears for his kindness. I didn't know how I could ever repay him. Tang did though. He gave Bruno one of his highest pitched happy barks ever. And had us both laughing.

We left Bruno at his cab and went inside. The place was just like a human hospital waiting room. There was a long counter looped with festive gold and red garlands, reminders of the season. Here, the hospital personnel registered patients and their families. In the center of the room were rows of vinyl covered seats where pet owners waited comforting their frightened pets.

Despite the time difference and the snowstorm, we had made it to our late afternoon appointment. A friendly young woman checked us in and asked us to take a seat. "Someone will come for you shortly."

I was wasted, emotionally exhausted and jet-lagged. Except for the Christmas decorations which seemed out of place with my mood, I didn't notice my surroundings too much. We weren't kept waiting more than fifteen minutes for which I was grateful. All I really wanted to do was get into a warm, soft bed and cuddle my dog.

"Marilee Christian?" Someone called, and I awoke from my thoughts.

A white-coated assistant smiled and indicated I follow him. I lifted Tang into my arms and we passed by a man carrying a tall cage containing a red and blue Macaw. I briefly wondered what was wrong with it and why it was here. But then something else caught my eye.

Waiting on a gurney was a German Shepard police dog. He was lying on his side with a large makeshift cloth bandage on his shoulder. Blood was seeping through the white cloth and a harried policeman was hovering over his canine partner, beside himself with grief as an intern came to take the dog to the OR.

I turned away from the tragic sight. *Please God. Let that dog live.*

I carried Tang close, my hands covering his eyes, into the examining room. I don't know if he smelled the wound, saw the blood or understood that the police dog had been shot while doing his job. I didn't want him to know and I didn't want him to see.

Tang glanced left and right, eyes pivoting as he took in the new environment, unaware as to what was going to happen next.

"Love the sweater," the assistant said, closing the door behind us.

Everyone did.

I must tell Eva when I got home.

A few minutes later, a very young female vet came in with a student who looked high-school aged but was probably college aged, and the male assistant left.

"I'm doctor Nichols," she said.

I swear, Dr. Nichols looked like she was barely out of university. But her manner spoke of professionalism and experience. "I hope you don't mind if one of our students sits in on this consultation."

"No, of course not," I said.

She was very cheerful as was the student vet. I wondered if cheerfulness was part of the core curriculum. The jobs these animal professionals had was serious indeed. Animals only came to the OVC if there was no other recourse. That meant their conditions were life and death.

"I explained to you over the phone the treatment for Tang's condition. We are hoping for a surgical cure, which means part of his lower jaw will be removed. Afterwards we'll test the bone to see if the extremities are free of cancer cells. If so, Tang probably won't need chemo or radiation therapy. We strongly believe this will be the case."

Her eyes were bright and she was smiling again.

I couldn't even begin to force an answering smile. My baby was going to be disfigured.

"We have excellent surgeons. I promise you; Tang will be able to eat and drink as normal after a few days."

I had no choice if I was to save Tang's life.

"Just one thing I wanted to ask," I said.

"Yes, of course." Dr. Nichols nodded agreeably.

"Tang is a very vocal little guy. He has this way of expressing his emotions where he lifts his head up and gives a happy howl." I paused, feeling trapped. Unable to really explain what I meant. "Will he still be able to do that?"

"I don't see why not." She gave me another reassuring nod.

When I had no more questions, and the vet was sure I understood the procedure, she passed me some papers to sign giving the surgeon permission to perform the procedure and the preop tests.

They took Tang to do the preliminary tests, and when he was done, they returned him to me with encouraging smiles.

Tang's response to all of their poking and prodding, x-rays and blood tests was a great big happy-bark of joy. He was nervous, but he trusted me. He even trusted all of the different technicians that had handled him. And for each of us there was always that howled song of joy.

"Tang will be assigned one of our student vets. In his case, Jolene here, who will stay with him following the surgery. Please try not to worry. He will never be alone. Our students hate for the animals to have to wear the e-collars around their necks so they prefer to stay with them all the time. And when the students are on a break, one of our assistants will be with him."

Yes, Tang hated those plastic cones. What pet didn't? Secretly I think they thought of it as the 'Cone of Shame.'

It wasn't even an hour when we left the hospital. Bruno was outside waiting for us as promised. His taxi smelled like French fries and vinegar, so he must have stood by his word and gone to some fast-food joint for dinner. He had an orange and brown A&W root beer paper cup in his cup holder.

Although I felt guilty for having asked him to wait, I don't believe I would have survived another minute waiting for a ride that might never come. The snowstorm had many people stranded, and the taxis were overwhelmed with requests. I greeted him with a grateful smile.

"Everything go okay?" he asked.

"Yes. As far as I know."

He drove us to the Delta Hotel where I had booked a room. I had no plans, except for room service and a good night's sleep.

"I will pick you up, tomorrow," Bruno said after he had removed my luggage from his car trunk and brought the suitcase and pet carrier inside the hotel lobby. Tang was not inside the carrier. The hotel was pet-friendly so Tang was trundling along at my feet.

"What time should I be here?" he asked.

Startled, I looked up from searching my purse for my credit card. He planned to return tomorrow? "No. You can't, Bruno," I objected. "You live in Toronto. I'll call a local cab."

"It's okay," he insisted. "Tomorrow is my day off. I will take you and my little *amico* to the hospital. You register and I will get the rest of your things."

What other things? I had only the one suitcase, my purse which was strapped across my chest, and Tang's carrier.

I shrugged as he walked away, and went inside.

Tang was eager to explore the new digs.

The lobby was opulent. The color palate was black and white with pot lights in the high ceilings, and here and there pendulum lights leading to the elevators. A large Christmas tree stood off to one side decorated in silver, white and black glass balls. The garlands were silver as were some very large jingle bells. And the twinkle lights were white.

The black reception counter rose up from cream and gray tiled floors. On the wall behind the counter hung intermittent white wreaths with red berries and bows. I leaned over the white marble countertop and signed the register and accepted the keycard. By that time, Bruno had returned with an A&W paper bag. He handed it to me and I opened it. Inside was a hamburger, French fries and a root beer. Still hot. Except for the drink. That was cold.

"You are too kind, Bruno."

"I have a dog too. And a wife and two kids. I know what you are feeling. You must eat. *Ciao ciao*. See you tomorrow."

I wanted to cry.

The hotel room was decorated in similar colors to the lobby. Mostly black and white but with splashes of color like yellow and blue in the chair cushions and accent pillows. There were white variegated poinsettias on the end table and the dresser. I set my luggage down on the floor and my dinner on the dresser. The smell of hamburger and fries was making my mouth water. Best to eat before it got cold.

But first I had to feed Tang. He hadn't eaten in hours due to the flight, the taxi trip and the vet appointment. I removed his sweater from over his head to a crackle of static. He didn't seem to notice. What he did notice was the food I was preparing. I dug out his plastic bowl and his bag of kibble from my large suitcase, and shook out a half cup. Then I placed it in front of him on the floor and watched him gobble it up. That took him probably thirty seconds to consume. Seems none of today's events had affected his appetite. I filled his bowl with water and collapsed on the bed. That would be his last meal before the surgery.

My mom should be home from the hospital now. I called her. I hadn't had time to talk to her when we landed at Pearson Airport because I was in a rush to get to Guelph and the vet appointment. As the phone rang, I reached for the A&W bag.

"Hi, Mom. It's me. Are you home? I just called to let you know we're in Guelph at the hotel."

The background on my Facetime screen was white. Could be her condo or a hospital corridor. Mom's face was slightly distorted from holding the phone too close.

"Oh, honey. No, I'm still at the hospital. Will be here for another hour. I wish you could have stopped over in Toronto for the night. But I understand. Tomorrow is Tang's surgery?"

"Yes. We'll come and visit you on our way back." Providing everything went according to plan and there were no complications.

"I should have found a way to come and pick you up," Mom insisted.

"You're a busy surgeon, and head of staff. You can't. You wouldn't still be at work right at this moment if you didn't have to be. We'll be fine." I was sitting on the bed with Tang, now comfortably satiated, wedged in between the multiple pillows. I held my cellphone in one hand and opened the A&W bag with the other. I pinched a French fry and popped it into my mouth. Then located the little packets of vinegar and ketchup and tried to tear them open with my teeth.

"I'm not worried about Tang," she said. "I know he'll be fine. It's you I'm worried about. It's not that I don't love Tang too, but you need to get out more. You need to meet someone."

The ketchup packet ripped and released an ooze of tomatoey salty-sweetness that fortunately fell over the fries instead of my lap. My luck with the vinegar was somewhat sloppier. A sting of acid hit me in the nose. But the liquid condiment was clear, so the dribbles that went onto the duvet were invisible. I rolled a fry into the wet spot and popped it into my mouth, decided that was not the solution, and quickly snatched a few tissues from the nightstand to mop it up.

"Now is not the time, Mom."

"I know. But a career and a dog isn't a full life."

I stuffed a few more fries into my mouth.

"You should talk," I answered between chews and swallows. "When was the last time you went out on a date?"

Her face wavered back and forth. "I don't have time."

I laughed despite myself. Famous last words. That was always the excuse. For both of us. Well, maybe I would have time now. Now that I was likely going to be unemployed. My mind drifted to Joel. But I had no idea if Joel was even interested in me that way. I had no job to go back to. So why would he want to date me? Besides, we lived on opposite sides of the country. It would never work.

"Mari?"

"Yes?"

The background of white was swishing by several closed doors and an elevator. She was on her way through the corridor to see a patient. "Is there something else bothering you?"

I shook my head, although she wasn't looking. "No. Don't worry about me. I'll talk to you tomorrow. After Tang's operation."

"Get some sleep," she said.

"G'night, Mom."

I disconnected the call and reached for the burger. I finished it before it turned completely cold.

I lay down on the bed beside my sweet boy. But there was no sleep for me that night.

CHAPTER 11

Bruno was there first thing in the morning, as promised. What a sweetheart. He had only just met us and was so kind as to spend his day off taxiing us to the hospital.

Although the squall from last night had stopped, the aftermath was quite apparent. Snow covered every inch of ground. The sidewalks were yet to be shoveled with spreading black footprints going every which way. The streets were slick and slushy, churned up by ongoing traffic, and dirty and greasy in places. Trees along the roadside were coated in thick layers of crystalline white.

Tang had no idea what was about to happen to him. He was just as bright-eyed and bushy-tailed as always.

I checked in at the counter. He was wearing his royal blue sweater and I was about to remove it when I was told to leave it on.

"We'll keep it with his other things," the

receptionist said.

It tore my heart in two as I handed him over to the veterinary assistant who had come to take him from me. "Don't worry," she said.

It was impossible to count the number of times people had said that to me. How could I not worry?

My baby was about to undergo radical surgery.

I could barely keep the tears from streaming down my face as I watched my tiny Tang, still dressed in his royal blue sweater, in the assistant's arms. He twisted his little head to watch me leave, his soft brown eyes questioning rather than frightened. Was this the last time I would ever see him?

"Be good, baby," I whispered. "Mummy will see you soon."

I hoped.

In some ways I guess I was grateful that Bruno had come to pick us up at the hotel. He was waiting outside for me now to take me back. It would be hours before Tang was out of surgery and in recovery. The thought of him undergoing such a radical procedure made me feel ill. But all of the specialists I had consulted said the same thing. It was the only way to save his life.

I don't know what I would have done had Bruno not been there to take me home. He saw the tragedy on my face and gently touched my shoulder. Just when you lose faith in all humanity, someone—a stranger—comes along and restores your faith.

No words were necessary. He could see that I was unable to talk.

"Everything will be okay," he said as he let me out at my hotel.

I must try my best to believe him.

When I got to my floor, I almost forgot to leave the elevator. I was that distracted. I apologized to the guests that were waiting to board and got out of their way then found my room. I was so agitated I couldn't get the keycard to work. After several tries, a chambermaid leaving the room next door, took pity on me.

"Sometimes they can be tricky," she said. She tapped the card on the sensor and it opened on the first try.

"Thank you," I mumbled.

Once inside, I crumpled onto the bed and felt the tears trickle down my cheeks to my jaw. I had no energy to wipe my eyes, and let the tears fall. Until there were none left. Why did crying make you feel like a used teabag?

Five tissues later, I took out my phone to call Jonny. My brother had asked me to keep him updated and I hadn't spoken to him since the night of that ill-fated Christmas party. While at the hospital I had turned off the volume of my ringer. The last thing I wanted were phone calls. Now I saw that I had several messages.

One was from Mom and one was from Jonny. The last message was from Mr. Hancock.

I ignored Mr. Hancock's message. I just could not deal with him right now.

Mom's message was warm and uplifting telling me that things had a way of working out.

Johnny's was the same. *Sometimes bad things happen before good things can.*

I collapsed crosswise onto the bed, my knees hanging over the edge. Why was my world crumbling around me? Sarah would have long since done my presentation for me. She would have either hit or missed. There was no other option. Mr. Hancock would have noticed my absence. I could just imagine the fury my no-show would have caused. He would have had little choice but to allow Sarah the stage.

There was no air in my lungs. I could not breathe. Could a person expire from an overdose of anxiety?

How could I bring myself to call Mr. Hancock?

Turns out, I didn't have to. He called me.

"Marilee?"

"Yes," I said, forcing my breathing to regulate. Breathing was supposed to be an involuntary, automatic response. Why did I feel like I had forgotten how?

The dread was unbearable. My heart palpitated and my palms perspired.

"You missed the meeting."

"Yes, I know, Mr. Hancock." There was no point in trying to plead my case. He knew why I had failed to appear to deliver the presentation.

"How is your dog?'

"I don't know yet. He's just gone into surgery." I probably wouldn't hear anything for hours.

His silence was short. "Your assistant did a good job of the pitch."

"I'm glad. I knew she was ready." Boy did I know it.

There was a long moment of quiet and I braced myself for what was coming. How could I blame him. Really.

"You realize, I meant what I said?"

There was no going back on his word. It would make him look weak.

I nodded, although the gesture was invisible. He took my silence as an acknowledgement.

"When you return, I want you to clean out your office." His voice was quiet. Sad. Not angry. I had disappointed him. Worse. I had failed him.

"Yes, Mr. Hancock."

There was nothing else to say. He hung up and I stared at my phone until it went black. Then I placed it on the nightstand and sat on the edge of the mattress like a zombie.

I don't believe I fully realized what I had done until that moment. I was too emotionally and physically exhausted to have argued with him. He had said nothing unexpected. Simply given me fair warning.

Did I have any recourse? Probably not. I had

backed out of my obligations. I was an executive and had no union to represent me, and I had no energy or will to sue him.

What was I going to do? I would lose my luxury townhouse, my car and have to live on my savings until I landed another job. Life was going to be hard. I tried to remember again Jonny's words. *Sometimes bad things happened before good things could.*

What good could possibly come out of this?

I must get out of here. Staying alone in this hotel room would drive me bonkers. And lead to nothing but self-pity and more tears. What could I possibly do that would be an effective distraction?

Shopping. It was Christmas. I needed to go shopping. Even if I didn't feel like it.

Bruno had gone home to Toronto. He made me promise to call him when it was time to pick up Tang. I couldn't impose on him to drive me to the mall. Besides, he was already halfway to the city.

When I asked the local cab driver where a nice shopping experience would be, he suggested the Old Quebec Street Mall. "It's like an indoor village," he said. "Very unique."

He wasn't lying. Both in history and atmosphere the place was like an indoor European market with elegant stone architecture and glass ceilings. As I walked down the main mall, I felt like I was strolling along an ancient street in Jolly Old England. Thanks to the open roof, the place was flooded with natural light, and signs hung from over the shops with mullioned windows and balconies overlooking the central avenue. Shoppers sat at patios on wooden benches or small round tables, sipping coffee and hot chocolate, amidst a swirl of festive activities like Christmas carolers, face painters, and Santa and his elves.

It was all so pretty and cheery that I almost turned back. A young family dressed in snowflake-spangled scarves and puffy parkas came out of a candy shop with oversized candy canes in multiple colors. The children were beaming and the parents were laughing and I thought how can they be so happy when my life is in despair?

My phone suddenly rang. Adrenalin shot through my body as a notion dawned on me. Had something happened to Tang? Oh my God. I almost didn't answer it.

But it wasn't the hospital. I raised my phone unsteadily to my ear.

"Hello, Sarah," I said. The caller ID had given me a heads-up as to who was calling. I swallowed my emotion and tried to sound normal.

"Marilee," she said. "I just wanted to let you know that everything went great. Les Malt was thrilled with the presentation. I got us the account."

What. No 'Hi, boss?' She usually called me that in a joking but affectionate way. I waited a breathless, few seconds for my heart to return to normal, and my breathing to stabilize.

"Good," I answered. I struggled with my thoughts. Being distracted did strange things to the brain. It was hard to come back from it.

"Isn't it wonderful?" Her voice was annoyingly filled with gaiety.

For you, sure. Then I had a thought. Funny thing; Mr. Hancock had said that Sarah had done a good job of the presentation, but not that she had won the account. Did that mean something?

I must ask. "When do you sign?"

She hesitated for a split second. "Soon."

Soon was very vague.

"You haven't set a date?"

"Well, no. But she said she'd be in touch."

And that could mean anything.

"Was there a verbal agreement?"

"How is Tang?" she asked to quickly change the subject.

I was caught off-guard, and emotionally preoccupied, not to mention distraught—so I answered her question. "I'm still waiting to hear. I dropped him off just over an hour ago. The surgery was scheduled for noon."

"I'm sure he'll be fine."

"I hope so."

Silence. And then she asked, "When will you be coming back?"

So, Mr. Hancock had kept my dismissal to himself. Well, I was too depressed to tell her the good news. But that also meant he hadn't automatically given her my job.

"I'm not sure… How was your date with Joel Joseph?" I asked to avoid answering specifically. Why did I ask that? Did I really want to know? The answer to that question might be the last straw. My heart already felt like it had been eaten by my stomach.

Sarah hesitated. An easy question. Good, bad, indifferent. How I wished it were the last two.

"How did you know about that?" she asked.

"I ran into him on the flight over. He was on his way home to Toronto."

I hoped the fact that Joel lived in Toronto would deter her from pursuing him.

"He told you we went out for dinner after the party?"

Dinner? No, he did not say that.

"Ah," I stumbled. "He said you went out."

"Yes, we did. And it was wonderful. I think we might have a connection. It was amazing."

After one date?

I was really getting frustrated. What right did I have to be upset? Except that at the moment almost anything might upset me. Joel was a nice man. He had actually never shown any sign that he was interested in me romantically. I was the one that had initiated most of our conversations. He was just being polite. And kind, because that was the type of person he was.

Sarah on the other hand. Her involvement with

Joel had me squirming. How could he find her interesting, appealing or attractive? After what she had done to me? He knew she had spun a tall tale about Les Malt owning a horse and being heartbroken at having to put it down. He was the one who had poked the hole in her story. She had lied. Had she not stabbed me in the back and if my feelings for Joel were platonic, I might have wished them well. Before all of this, I had thought Sarah a helpful, considerate, clever person. All traits that Joel might like. And the conniving part? I sighed. Truth was, that was a matter of opinion.

I replayed the Golden Rule of marketing to myself. *The people's emotions that mattered were the buyers. Clue into those and you had them where you wanted them.*

This applied to professional and romantic rivals as well.

There were people in the business world who would admire what Sarah had done. Taking advantage of a situation was different from cheating someone. She was looking out for number one. And that was not me.

Still, I would never have done that to her.

I had to exit this conversation before I said something I would regret.

"Look, Sarah, I have to go. I'm very tired. I'll see you when I get back."

CHAPTER 12

Tang's surgery was successful, but he wasn't out of the woods yet. He stayed at the hospital for three nights. During that time, my mom and Jonny kept me occupied by calling me three times a day.

I tried to contact Joel to update him on Tang's progress, but could never seem to get him at home. To be honest, I wanted to see if I could somehow twist the conversation so that I could find out if he had actually gone out for dinner with Sarah. I refused to take her word for it. But as I said, I got no answer.

Not wanting to be a pest, I refrained from leaving a message. Nor did I call his office. He had a busy practice. And if he was involved with Sarah, he had more than enough on his plate. He was also probably harassed trying to catch up after being away for almost a week.

Then again, maybe I was wrong about him.

Maybe he was just being nice when I met him in Vancouver, and then a few days later on the plane. He'd seemed so genuine. But what did I know? Some people were charmers, and that was all it was. Could it be that he was simply a charmer, and didn't mean a word of what he'd said? Or maybe he had no time to care about what happened to me or Tang. I disconnected the call after listening to it ring eight times.

Bruno called to make sure I was okay.

I was far from okay. Not until I got Tang home would I feel okay.

The veterinary students were wonderful. The girl, Jolene, who was assigned to Tang stayed by his side twenty-four hours a day. She called every evening to update me on his condition.

"He's looking around very interested in his surroundings," she said. "He's even walking about."

I laughed. That was Tang. Always curious. Always active.

When the doctors decided he could eat on his own, they let him go home. It was sunny that afternoon, the brilliance sparkling on the snow as Bruno drove me to the hospital. He insisted on coming because Tang had trapped him under his spell.

I asked Bruno to come inside with me. It was the least I could do after all his concern and kindness, and after driving all the way from Toronto to collect me. Besides, I was frightened to be alone.

"So nice to see you again, Marilee. I'm Jolene. We met briefly just before the surgery, and we've been chatting on the phone the last three nights."

"So nice to see *you* again," I said, sincerely meaning it. "Of course, I remember meeting you. And thank you for taking such good care of Tang."

"The surgeon will be here in a moment to speak with you," she said. She was carrying Tang in her arms.

His eyes looked bright. His mouth had been reconstructed and there were stitches in his jaw. His tongue protruded halfway out of his mouth. He wore a white cone around his neck. And a morphine patch on his back.

I shot a horrified glance at Bruno. But Bruno was smiling with relief that Tang was okay. In fact, Tang's tail was wagging under the student vet's arm.

But all I could think of was, what had I done to my dog? Would I ever get used to seeing him like that?

"He's doing very well," Jolene said. "He was a joy to look after."

"He's going to be fine?" Bruno asked.

"Oh, yes," she said, grinning. And handed him to me. "Everything went exactly as hoped. He came out of the anesthetic quickly, and without any negative effects."

Tang's soft fur nestled into my arms. I was

suddenly overcome with the reality that Tang had survived. How I wanted to bury my face in his, but the cone was in our way. I cuddled him as best I could without interfering with the patch or the cone. *Thank you, thank you, thank you!* Gratitude descended on me in a flood. Tang was going to live!

I hugged him gently against me. *Can we please just get out of here and go home?*

The door behind the student vet opened and the surgeon came in.

I nearly dropped Tang.

I could barely get the words out. "*You* did the surgery?"

Joel smiled at me. "And hello to you, too." He told Jolene it was fine for her to leave. I thanked her again, and then we were alone.

"I was a last-minute stand-in," Joel said. So that was why he had failed to answer my calls. He was busy operating on Tang. "Doctor Patali fell ill and didn't want to do the procedure when she wasn't at her best, so she called on me."

"Thank goodness you were available."

"It was Tang," he said with a grin.

But I knew he would have done it for any dog.

"So," he said. "The surgery went well. As you can see, the little fellow is quite alert and ready to go home. He's eating well. The stitches can come out in ten days."

I stared at Tang's small face. His tongue was hanging out of his mouth.

Joel noticed and said, "He'll learn to hold his tongue in. It might just take a little time." And smiled.

I managed to smile in return. "Oh, Joel, I can't thank you enough."

"My pleasure. And, by the way. The jawbone has been sent to the pathology lab. Results should be back in a few days. Where are you staying?"

"At the Delta hotel, but Bruno—Oh my gosh. Where are my manners? I am so sorry, Bruno." The cabbie had been waiting silently by my side as I conversed with Joel. I was about to say that Bruno would drive me and Tang to my mother's home. "Joel, this is Bruno, a wonderful man, who took care of me and Tang while we were in Guelph. He's a taxi driver from Toronto. But he is such an angel, and has been here with us through all of it. He is going to drive me and Tang to my mom's place in Toronto where we'll stay until we learn the outcome of the biopsy." I turned to Bruno. "And Bruno, please thank your wife for allowing you to do this."

"She's happy to let me help you. She wants you and Tang to come for dinner at our house one night."

"I would love that…. But I've gotten off-track. Bruno meet Joel. As you've learned, he's Tang's surgeon."

"Nice to meet you, Doc," Bruno said. "Great job you did on my little *amico*. Looks cute as ever."

"Thanks, Bruno. And it's a pleasure to meet you.

Any friend of Tang's is a friend of mine."

We all laughed at that.

"Bruno, would you mind if I spoke to Marilee privately for a moment?" Joel asked.

"No. Of course not. I shouldn't even be here. I will wait for you in the cab," he said, addressing me.

When Bruno was gone, Joel explained to me what would happen next with Tang. "Hopefully, we'll get an all clear from the lab. And if that is the case, we can declare a surgical cure. No further treatment will be necessary."

"And if it's not? What happens then?"

"Then there are several options, two of which are radiation therapy and chemotherapy. Dogs generally respond well to either. And the side effects are minimal or negligible. They seem to be tougher than us humans." He grinned.

I was silent.

"But no need to worry about that yet. All you need to do now is give him soft foods for the next few days and plenty of water. Let him sleep if he wants to."

"How long before we know?" I asked.

"I've put a rush on it. Should only take a few days."

I looked down at my boy. He was quite comfortable in my arms and not agitated at all.

"Hey, Marilee. I—I have to apologize for not returning your calls."

Marilee. Not Mari?

He knew I had called? I left no messages. Then I remembered that smart phones displayed the names of missed calls even if you failed to leave a message.

"It's okay, Joel. You were busy. You have a practice of your own as well as helping out here at the hospital. And... and you have a personal life." Of which I was not a part. Was he really involved with Sarah? "I—I just wanted to keep you posted."

"It wasn't that," he said.

Silence. Before he continued. "I received some upsetting news when I got home. I had to get my act together to do a good job operating on Tang. Afterward, it took me awhile to adjust."

"I'm so sorry, Joel." He had done so much for me already. And here he was with problems of his own. "Can I ask what it was?" I should not have said that. If it was personal, it was none of my business.

He shrugged. "The reason I postponed returning your calls was... well, I knew you had enough things to worry about. And I didn't need an update on Tang since I was going to see him through all aspects of the procedure and recovery. But... the thing is... the thing that upset me, uh, in a way it affects you too."

Now I was really stumped. And more than a little concerned.

"What do you mean? What happened, Joel. Please tell me before I go crazy."

He gave me a small smile. "It has probably

affected you more than me. It's... Actually, it has nothing to do with me. It's my mother. She left Magnus. She wants a divorce."

I managed to swallow my gasp. So that was why Mr. Hancock had been so unreasonable. That was what those papers were on his desk!

"Oh dear. I had no idea."

"Why would you? *I* had no idea. My mother never mentioned she was having problems with her marriage. Or that she had met someone else. In fact, she thinks she's in love with the new guy. If that's the case..." he shrugged again. "It doesn't matter how I feel about it I suppose, since it's my mother's happiness that is at stake. But it's too bad. Because I really think Magnus is a good guy. He floated my loan when I graduated from veterinary college. Treated me like I was his own son. Without his help I wouldn't have been able to set up my own practice. I would have had to join someone else's. As it is I was able to set up my own clinic and hire a junior partner as well."

That *was* a good guy.

"Life is strange," I admitted. "I only wish that it wasn't infringing on your stepfather's happiness." And by default, my own.

"It won't affect my relationship with him. He's been the only father I've known since I was twelve. And she *doesn't* want it to affect my relationship with him." He waited to collect his thoughts. "She tells me they haven't been happy for years. I can't speak for Magnus, but if my mother wasn't happy then I can't imagine he was either."

Unhappy as divorce was, staying together in an unhappy marriage was worse. I should know. My parents had done the same thing.

I only hoped the drinking wasn't going to be an issue. I did not like associating Mr. Hancock with the constant reek of whiskey.

I nodded. "Thanks for telling me, Joel. It explains a lot."

"I thought it might."

CHAPTER 13

My mother's condo is in the St Lawrence neighborhood. It's a twelve-story boutique hotel in a heritage community near a massive farmer's market and garden park. She chose the location because it was in the Old Town section of Toronto where the charm of heritage buildings is reflected in all the new development.

"Your brother and I have been talking," Mom said as she stirred the marinara sauce in a large heavy-bottomed aluminum pot. She paused to drizzle in a cup of rich red wine, her secret ingredient, which really was no secret at all. The real secret was to use good wine, not the cheap stuff. "We've decided to have Christmas here instead of at Jonny's. That way Tang can recuperate without any messy flights."

I had reiterated my regrettable experience concerning our flight out. "Besides, we don't yet know what the next steps are for him," she added.

"And Eva is okay with that?"

"She says the kids are ecstatic about going somewhere with snow for Christmas."

My eyes drifted to the large picture window opposite the stainless-steel induction stove. The condo was on the tenth floor and was one of the low-rise's penthouse units. There were two of these units on the rooftop facing back-to-back, and they overlooked the neighborhood.

Sliding doors, caked with snow and ice, opened off the kitchen and the living room. With some effort I managed to loosen the kitchen door, slide it wide enough to step outside, and embraced the late afternoon chill in my oversized cowlneck sweater and fuzzy slippers. The door crunched shut behind me before Tang could follow. "Mummy will back in a minute," I mouthed.

He wagged his tail and stared through the glass at me with bright dancing eyes.

Mom's condo had a glorious view of a treed park with frozen ponds and creeks. The cedars and pines were crystalized with ice and the dark wet wood of the maple trees contrasted beautifully with their winter white sleeves. At night the park was illuminated with lights, and this year, some locals had decided to do their own version of the Festival of Lights.

Someone had refurbished an old sleigh and decked it out in green and red. Others made wire reindeer and entwined them in white lights. There was a lighted scene of Santa and his elves, and in a far corner was a makeshift manger displaying the Nativity scene. When Tang was completely back on his feet, I should take him to see it. He would love it. It had everything he adored. People and animals and a little baby.

On Mom's rooftop patio, potted blue spruces laced with snow, surrounded the flagstones where deck furniture remained waiting for the spring thaw. Sometimes Mom sat outside in cold weather bundled in her parka and blankets in front of the gas firepit. It was a wonderful invention, the patio firepit. It was primal and socially connecting all at once. And it was mandatory when the whole family was here for Christmas.

Yes, the kids would love it here. The place had three guest bedrooms, one of which Tang and I were currently occupying.

If snow was what the kids wanted, Toronto had no shortage of that.

I turned and saw that Tang was still standing in the same spot, wagging his tail and waiting for me. I laughed and went inside.

"What's the matter, baby boy? Did you think I'd abandoned you? I would *never* abandon you." I got down on my haunches and gave him a kiss on his head. The cone had been removed earlier today and it was clear it was unnecessary. I had also removed the morphine patch. He was no longer in pain. And the medicinal smell in his fur was totally gone.

Mom stopped stirring to retrieve a small festively beribboned and be-bowed gift basket of dog goodies from the marble island, and set it down in front of Tang. My quick eyes took note that the contents were all National Pet brand. My mother was nothing if not loyal to me and mine.

She edged the cellophane slightly from the wicker rim. Tang immediately shoved his snout in and started sniffing.

"Nothing wrong with his nose," she said.

"You know he can't eat any of that."

She nodded. "But in a few weeks, I'm sure he'll be able to enjoy some of it. Most of those treats are soft."

"Mom... thank you. You are wonderful..." I was close to tears again. "Everyone has been wonderful." Everyone that is except two people. Mr. Hancock and Sarah.

But I wasn't going to think about them today. No. I glanced around at my mom's beautiful condo, and the warmth and love that emanated from this room. Marinara sauce, Mom and Tang. Right now, God was in his heaven and all was right with the world.

The pot of water on the stove was beginning to roil and Mom lowered the heat to a gentle bubble. Then she went to the pantry to fetch the dried pasta.

"When will Jonny and the kids be able to fly

out?" I asked.

She opened the glass canister of spaghetti and removed a handful. "Not until school is over for Christmas vacation. What is it? Another week?"

"By that time, I should know the prognosis."

"Don't worry, darling. There are so many available treatments today. In fact, veterinary medicine is at the forefront of some of our most promising cancer treatments for humans."

I knew that. Joel had told me the same thing.

"Does Joel have any family here?" Mom asked, stirring the spaghetti into the boiling water.

"No. His mother and stepfather live in Vancouver. As for brothers and sisters. He never mentioned any."

"So, if he's alone, why don't you invite him for Christmas dinner?"

I had told her about my chance meeting with Joel, and how surprised I was to learn that he was a veterinary surgeon. And how shocked I was when I discovered he was the actual surgeon who had performed that miracle on Tang.

Mom returned to stirring the marinara, then handed me the sauce-coated spoon for a taste.

"He bears a remarkable resemblance to Jonny," I said, and licked the extra-long-handled, wooden utensil.

"Seriously?"

I nodded and set the spoon on the spoon rest. "That's how we met. Tang thought he was Jonny."

Mom laughed, waving some steam out of her face. "And he lives in this big city, alone? He sounds like the ideal man. You must invite him for Christmas... Enough oregano?"

"Oh, I'm sure he won't be alone. And yes, the sauce is perfect."

I mean what did I know about Joel's personal life? For all I knew he had a girlfriend. I only hoped that his special someone wasn't Sarah. Yes, I was jealous. Or maybe it was more resentment. She was stealing everything from me (including my favorite earrings!), but none of it was really her fault. And Joel wasn't mine to steal. Still, the thought made me feel bad. How do I even describe in words that feeling? Empty somehow, and deflated.

But it was fun to dream.

How amazing would that be if Dr. Joseph joined us for Christmas dinner?

CHAPTER 14

It was a long wait to find out the results of the biopsy. Even though Joel had said it would only be a few days. But after five days I was beginning to wonder exactly how Joel defined 'a few days.' The hospital was silent, and so was he.

When the wait began to threaten my sanity—a week had gone by—I called the hospital.

The receptionist who answered told me she would call back when she had spoken to the attending vet. Dare I phone Joel at his practice? My patience was wearing thin. Without news—soon—I would go insane. Yes, that was an overstatement.

The hospital staff was kind but how could they possibly understand what I was feeling? Would I be overstepping the boundaries if I called Joel myself?

Mom was at work, and again I was alone with my brain. I had to get outside and find some fresh air. My mind was eating itself with all the worrisome thoughts. And the waffling. If the cancer had spread... *Stop it!*

I decided to go to the St. Lawrence Market and obtain some fresh groceries for Mom. The streets were bustling and most of the sidewalks had been cleared of snow. Icy humps continued to obstruct the curbside, and I was careful to step over these. The last thing I needed was a sprained ankle or a broken leg from a slip and fall.

Tang wanted to come but he needed to have some quiet time to recuperate. I had coaxed him into the oversized crate filled with soft pillows and blankets, and latched the door. Sweetie that my mother was, she had bought the crate for Tang knowing we'd have a layover for several days.

Normally Tang was not crated when I was out. But he was still mending, and I couldn't risk him hurting himself in my absence. At this very moment, he was probably wondering why I had locked him in jail.

The large brick building housing the market was in the center of Old Town. It was festively decorated with lights and large, green, live holly boughs caught up in colorful ribbon. It is one of the largest markets of its kind in the world. There were more than 120 vendors and artisanal shops ranging from fresh fruits and vegetables, and locally grown hothouse berries to every kind of meat, bread and cheese you could imagine. Not to mention flowers, houseplants and local crafts. There were some handstitched, Christmas teddy bear pillows I was tempted to buy. Alas, I had come here for food, not knickknacks.

The smells of smoked fish and sausage, mingled with the scents of newly cut flowers and fresh baked sweets. Cinnamon, ginger spice and candy smells drifted at me. Mom needed parmesan cheese, a newly-baked baguette, and multicolored heirloom tomatoes and fresh basil for dinner tonight. The plan was to have leftover pasta.

As I wove through the tight aisles with my purchases, I caught sight of a familiar figure. She was dressed in a red wool coat with a black scarf, and black high-heeled boots, quite striking amidst the more casually dressed shoppers, myself included. I was wearing my old, pale blue, puffy parka, with a tuque over my unwashed hair.

I had to blink a couple of times to be sure I wasn't seeing things.

There was nothing wrong with my eyes. I even removed my sunglasses to be sure.

It was Sarah. And the colors she was wearing reminded me of the dress—the red, black and silver dress—she had worn to the Christmas party. My hands flew to my ears. Since my arrival in Ontario, I had forgotten to wear earrings.

Sarah had my Silver Bells. I had to get them back.

What was she doing in Toronto? I just spoke to her a few days ago. The day of Tang's surgery. She never mentioned anything about coming out to

Toronto.

I was about to weave through the multiple stalls to reach her when a man carrying two paper cups of coffee left a beverage stand and approached her. She turned and I could see that it was indeed Sarah Phipps. My Sarah Phipps. The man who handed her a coffee was also familiar. He had his back to me but I recognized the fisherman knit sweater and the height and build. From the back, he could have been my brother. Except for the fisherman knit, which he would never wear. Because of the crewneck.

It wasn't Jonny. He and his family were due to arrive the day after tomorrow. Besides, why would he be meeting Sarah?

It could only be one person. And that was Joel. I hadn't spoken to Joel since the day at the hospital. He had promised to call as soon as he received the results of the biopsy. I never bothered him at his clinic because I knew he would have called if he had news. Besides, with his busy practice he'd have to avoid mere chitchat.

Apparently, I was wrong.

Because here he was having coffee with Sarah.

They were so absorbed in each other that they missed the woman three stalls down in pale blue (yeah me) staring at them with her groceries dangling from two hemp bags in her left hand, and a half-eaten sandwich in her right. I should go up to them and say hello. But how could I?

Joel never mentioned that he was serious about

Sarah. They met, what? Just over a week ago? How could anything have developed between them in so short a time?

I felt sick. Partly because I was still anxious about Tang. But mostly because this was so unexpected.

Joel's love life was his own business. He was my dog's veterinary surgeon. He was obligated to report to me only the things that concerned Tang.

Obviously, he had received no news or he would have called.

He certainly wouldn't be having a coffee break with Sarah.

Or would he?

The peameal bunwich I had bought for my late lunch tasted dry and mealy in my mouth. I chewed what was left on my tongue. And swallowed. Ordinarily it would have been delicious, but now... I tossed the remainder into a trash bin.

I searched for the exit and made a beeline for the outdoors.

I dodged getting hit by a car and ended up with slush on my knees. I clutched the grocery bags to my chest and heard the air gush out of my puffy jacket.

The snow squeaked under my boots.

When I arrived home, I was breathing hard but calmer. I unlocked the door expecting to be greeted with an empty house. I got the surprise of my life. Eva and the kids were there. They had released

Tang from jail and now I received some heartfelt tail-wags. He hadn't given me a happy bark yet. I was worried that his happy bark days were over. But maybe he was still recuperating and lacked the energy.

"Auntie Mari, Auntie Mari. Is Tang going to be okay?"

"I explained a little about what was going on," Eva said.

I was grateful for that. Explaining to children life's ups and downs, especially the downs, were not in my skill set.

"He's going to be fine," I said. "Look at how happy he is to see you!"

That satisfied them and they returned to playing with Tang.

"Is he?" Eva whispered.

I nodded. "So far, so good. Still waiting on the results of the biopsy, but the surgeon is confident." I lowered my voice. "Truth be told. The waiting—is driving me crazy."

Eva gave me a hug.

"Where's Jonny?" I asked releasing her.

"He's gone to book us rooms in a hotel. We don't want to overwhelm your mom. Besides, she wasn't expecting us for three more days. But Jonny dropped us off with the key." She sat down to rub her feet. "Airplanes always make my feet swell up."

"Put your feet up." I shoved the ottoman towards her. "You should have told us you were arriving today. I could have gotten your rooms ready."

She slumped back, wriggling her toes. "Airlines had a mix-up with overbooking. It was either today or late next week. That would take us to after Christmas. So, no time to call. Had to pack and go." She grinned and flopped back against the armchair she was seated in."

She glanced at Tang. "When do you expect to hear from the hospital?"

I shook my head, then explained the current situation to Eva. And while the kids sat on the floor and cuddled Tang, I waited for the phone to ring.

A call came from the hospital within the hour. Eva gestured for me to take the phone into my bedroom. The kids were making too much noise. She went to settle them down and I closed the door.

I held my breath trying to keep the anxiety out of my tone, then said, "Hello?"

"I'm sorry Ms. Christian," the med tech said. "The pathologist is away for a convention. He should return by tomorrow. We'll fast-track the results. You should know by late tomorrow afternoon."

CHAPTER 15

The wait was agonizing. But at least it gave me something to think about other than the fact that Joel and Sarah were dating. It also explained Joel's silence. He had no news.

When Jonny came from checking the luggage into the hotel suite, he was dressed in a holiday sweater of green and red. "It's to disguise the marinara spatters, he said with a grin. You know how I am about Mom's sauce."

I did indeed. It was a staple from when we were kids. And in case you're worried about the wine, alcohol evaporates when cooked. So, no, we weren't under-aged boozehounds.

There was so much left over when she made it last week that we were having it again. Good thing, because the unexpected number of dinner guests would have been quite flustering. Since Mom's work at the hospital could be erratic, and I was a disaster when it came to cooking for more than two, the already prepared sauce, now in the freezer in three batches, was a lifesaver. We'd need all three of those batches tonight.

So, as I was saying, hail to the mighty marinara sauce. Jonny's kids loved Mom's marinara too. But then, what kid said no to spaghetti?

When Mom got home, she was overjoyed to see her family altogether. We gathered around the table and dug in to a delicious Italian feast. In anticipation of the news tomorrow I drank a bit too much wine at dinner.

The hospital called late in the afternoon. I was all nerves. Tang was feeling quite well and happy and was back to bouncing around, and giving me kisses with his long, lolling tongue. Eva and the twins had returned after spending the night in the hotel with Jonny. The plan was for Jonny's family to stay in the hotel for a couple of nights and then return on Christmas Eve to spend the next four days with Mom. With her work schedule, it made their visit a little less hectic.

I left Tang in the living room with the kids and took the phone into my bedroom.

"Good news Ms. Christian. The results of the biopsy are in. There is no evidence of cancer on the periphery of the bone. Dr. Joseph will contact you personally when he's free. I called his office. He's in surgery at the moment."

"Thank you," I said, and burst into tears.

Mom just happened to poke her head into my bedroom at the moment. She had just come home from work. She shot through the half-opened door and cried, "Mari, honey, what's happened? Has the cancer spread?" She gathered me in her arms and I sobbed on her shoulder like a baby.

Eva must have heard something and popped her head in.

Mom shook her head and waved her away. Eva took the cue and shut the door before returning to the living room.

I shook my head, realizing she'd got it all wrong, but I was having trouble getting the words out. "No. No. Tang's okay. They got it all. He's cancer free. Let me go and tell Eva, before she upsets the kids."

Mom laughed. "You silly goose. You scared me." She released me and added, "Don't worry, Eva won't say anything to the twins."

I accepted the tissue box she retrieved from the end table. And snapped out several to mop my eyes and blow my nose. I still felt so befuddled. "I'm sorry. I am just so relieved. I can't stop crying." And laughed through my tears.

"Well, that's something to celebrate."

It really was.

She stood watching me while I pulled myself together. When I rejoined the family, I wanted to radiate happiness, not this messy muddle of emotions. I especially wanted my boy to know how much I loved him.

The tissue box was empty, so that was my cue to follow Mom out the door. But I needed one more minute. Just one more minute to clear my head.

I desperately wanted to call Joel to thank him again for saving my dog's life. But I realized my irrational burst of emotion was not just because of Tang, but the results of pent-up feelings that I had been guarding for weeks.

Sarah still had my Silver Bell earrings. Why was I thinking about that? And Joel hadn't phoned or even sent word via text or email. More impersonal, sure. But maybe that was how he felt. He was Tang's surgeon. I was Tang's mom. There was no romantic entanglement.

Now, I had even more reason to wait until he called.

CHAPTER 16

Joel never did call. I guess he figured the hospital had reported the good news. The girl at the Ontario Veterinary College hospital asked if I could bring Tang to Guelph to have his stitches removed as that was where Dr. Joseph would be doing his surgeries until Christmas. Apparently, Tang's original surgeon, Dr. Patali was still ill with Covid, but on the road to recovery and refused to return to work prematurely in case she infected the other staff members.

Why hadn't he called me himself? I knew he was busy, but I was disappointed.

Despite my chaotic feelings, I really admired Joel for stepping in to help out. His partner would be busy doing double time while Joel was at the OVC.

I was a little nervous about seeing Joel again. I was afraid I might act weird. But nothing could destroy my mood today. Bruno had offered to take us back to Guelph when I texted him the good news about Tang's biopsy.

"You look *fantastico*," he said stooping to play with Tang outside the hospital doors.

Tang really did look good. He was back to his old self, prancing about and jumping on everyone and wagging his tail like a maniac. The only thing he hadn't done yet was his happy bark.

"Come inside with us," I suggested.

"No, no," Bruno said. "It is a busy hospital. I don't want to take up room. I'll wait here. You won't be long if it is just to remove the stitches."

"Okay," I said. "See you in a bit."

What a different day this was from the day we had arrived from Vancouver. No blizzard today. The sun was shining; the sky was a clean blue with just some wispy swirls of white. I hadn't had time to check the forecast but nothing could change my mood. If it was going to snow, then let it snow!

The Christmas decorations outside and inside the hospital seemed vitally appropriate on this glorious day.

Tang was happy too, strutting around like a show dog. Though what kind of show would want a dog with a tongue constantly hanging out of his mouth! Who cared. He was alive and healthy and thriving!

But it wasn't that way for everyone, I realized as I sat us down to wait. There was a girl beside me with her grandfather and a kennel containing two ferrets. The girl, no more than fifteen or sixteen, looked like she had lost her best friend. Her world had crashed down around her, and she was perilously close to losing hope.

Ten days ago, that was me. And now look at us. Tang, wearing his blue sweater, despite the surgical alteration to his face, looked adorable. He had a whole new life ahead of him.

A desperate need to reassure the girl came over me. What could I say? I knew when I was in that situation, nothing short of a miracle could lift my spirits.

"This is a wonderful hospital," I said. "They'll take good care of them." The ferrets seemed overly large around the belly, and I asked if they were pregnant.

"No," she said tearfully. "They have adrenal disease."

I had no idea what adrenal disease was, but it was clearly serious. The ferrets wouldn't be at the OVC otherwise.

The front door suddenly opened bringing in a blast of cold air. A man walked in. I wouldn't have noticed him in particular except that he seemed familiar. He was dressed in a tan overcoat with a stylish cashmere scarf around his neck, and dress slacks beneath the coat. He wore thick leather gloves and a matching beret. What's more, he had no pet with him.

Did he work here?

He looked like high-level admin. He went to the reception counter and spoke to one of the staff members, and then he turned and came towards the waiting area.

I almost choked when I recognized him. It was Mr. Hancock. What was he doing in Guelph? What was he doing at the OVC?

Then it hit me. Joel. His stepson was temporarily working at the hospital.

I lowered my eyes. Maybe he didn't see me. What could I say to him? The situation was awkward and I wished he would go away.

He sat down on the other side of the girl with the ferrets and her grandfather.

"Sick pets?" I heard him say.

Did Mr. Hancock really care? Or was he only making friendly conversation to pass the time? It was his way. I had seen him charm clients in that manner and I guess it had become a habit even outside the office.

The grandfather grunted. He had driven his granddaughter to the hospital. So clearly, he loved her. But he wore an impatient expression on his face that said: 'They're only animals.'

It was the exact same expression I had seen on Mr. Hancock's face the day I had asked him for sympathy leave.

My eyes took in all of the concerned and heartbroken people in this place. I remembered the macaw and the bleeding police dog from our first visit. I prayed they had all been saved, just like my dog had been.

Only animals? Never!

Tang agreed. The girl and her grandfather were called into the examining room with her two beloved ferrets and I wished her well. Tang trundled over to where Mr. Hancock was sitting. In spite of the stitches under his mouth, he gave his defining happy howl of joy.

Involuntarily I beamed. Even Mr. Hancock couldn't stay grumpy with Tang around. He actually cracked a smile.

"That dog never stops wagging his tail," he remarked.

He looked over and realized it was me.

"Hello Mr. Hancock," I said.

For two seconds he was silent. Then he said, "Marilee. My apologies. I didn't see you there." He looked down at my dog who gazed up at him with adoring eyes. And wagged his tail. Another happy bark escaped before I could answer.

We both laughed. We couldn't help it. Me because I was so ecstatic that Tang had finally found his happy voice again. And Mr. Hancock because… well I don't know why. Except that Tang's howl of ultimate joy could only make you smile.

And it did.

"You are one cheery fella, aren't you?"

I gently tugged him away. "I'm sorry if he's bothering you."

"He isn't," Mr. Hancock said. He scratched Tang on the rump and Tang spun in ecstasy. Mr. Hancock's eyes studied Tang's reconstructed mouth, the lolling tongue, and the skillful stitching around his jaw. He returned his attention to me and said, "I'm glad to see the surgery went well."

"Thank you." I raised my head but couldn't quite bring myself to meet his gaze. "Please forgive me for letting you down, Mr. Hancock."

Magnus Hancock's eyes went back to Tang. Tang was watching all the people coming and going and all the pets that had arrived for treatment. His eyes were bright with curiosity and excitement, and everyone who made eye contact with him got a tail wag and a happy howl.

"A little social butterfly, aren't you?"

"He loves people. He loves animals."

Apparently, he even loves you.

Mr. Hancock's eyes sought mine, and I struggled to meet them. For the first time I saw regret and compassion in his face. "You have nothing to be sorry for. I actually came to see Joel, but I was hoping he could tell me where to find you."

"You wanted to find me?"

He nodded. "I know I could have phoned. But I wasn't sure you'd want to speak to me."

"I don't hold a grudge against you, Mr. Hancock. Of course, I would speak to you."

"Well, then, will you do me a favor? And call me Magnus. I think we've known each other long enough to be on a first name basis."

"Of course." Although it might take me awhile. I had never called him Magnus. Never even thought of him as Magnus. To me he was always Mr. Hancock. The boss.

A thought struck me. Why should I call him Magnus? This was probably the last time I would ever see him. Then another thought occurred to me. He wanted to speak to me? And before I could check myself, I blurted, "Is something wrong? Did Sarah not nail the account?"

"Oh, she nailed it."

"Then what's the problem?"

"Apparently, she has been spreading tales about you."

I frowned. Why would she do that? I had practically given her my job.

"It was something about a horse. That you made up some story about Les Malt's horse. That she was going to euthanize it." Ah, right. The EveryPet Emporium's Chief Purchasing Officer.

"Les Malt was outraged that you were making up stories about her. After Sarah arranged for the contract to be signed, Les found out about the rumor. She was furious that someone in the company was rumormongering about her. No matter how harmless. She's a stickler for privacy. I should have told you. Your assistant, Sarah knew. I enlightened her myself. I thought it would make her more cautious. She seemed to have a knack for connecting with people, so I engaged her to be my ears and eyes. I was wrong."

Sarah was an industrial spy? Okay, I was exaggerating. That wasn't exactly what Hancock had said. But he did say he had recruited her to screen the rumor mill.

"Les Malt and my wife—well, now my ex-wife—"

"You have my sympathies, Mr. Hancock." Had that come out too quickly?

"Magnus."

"Mr—I mean Magnus." I smiled.

"And no need for sympathy. Natalia and I have drifted apart. *She* apparently, farther apart than me. She's in Hawaii for the holidays."

My brows shot up but I kept my mouth closed.

"Her mother in Calgary recovered. That wasn't a lie." I never meant to accuse him of one. "She decided to continue on to Hawaii and celebrate Christmas there." With her new beau?

"Natalia and Les are college friends. They go a long way back and are very close. They tell each other everything. I worried about losing the account. I knew that Les would support Natalia. Which was why I didn't want you to offend her in any way, not even by requesting a reschedule of the presentation... That was a mistake." He glanced down at Tang. "She called me up later in the week accusing me of sending a spy into her midst. She said if that was how we did business she wanted nothing to do with us. The rumor indicated that the spy was you."

I allowed Mr. Hancock to continue until he was finished. Didn't even try to defend myself. I had nothing left to lose. Sarah's lies could not touch me now.

He was quiet.

"She doesn't have a horse," I said.

"I know."

I shrugged. None of this had anything to do with me.

"Joel contacted me."

Ah, so that was how he knew.

"Sarah is no longer in my employ."

My eyebrows rose. "Mr. Hancock—"

"Magnus."

"Magnus. Please don't fire her on my account."

"She is deceitful."

"I don't think she meant to be. I think she's just young. And a little cocky. But definitely ambitious." And besides hadn't he recruited her to listen to other people's conversations?

He read my mind. "That was also a mistake. I never meant for Sarah to make up stories about people, especially not about her supervisors or potential clients. All I asked her to do was to report anything of interest that would give the company an advantage in negotiations."

I understood. It was how one did business.

Perhaps it wasn't all her fault. Maybe she had

misunderstood.

"I made a mistake trusting her to give me relevant information. You know, they aren't kidding when they say it's lonely at the top. Half the time I have no idea what is going on in my own company. Especially when it comes to people I rely on. I needed someone on the ground floor, and she convinced me she was the person. And while I trusted her to bring me information, I did not trust her to win a big client. Turns out I was wrong on both counts."

"Sarah is very talented," I said, begrudgingly.

"Why are you defending her?" he asked.

Yes. Why was I?

Maybe because of Tang. If there was one thing this whole ordeal with Tang had taught me was that we should be more like him. He was still wagging his tail at everyone who came near or even just got out of their seat to take their pet in to be examined. Lucky people. They even got a happy bark for simply making eye contact.

Tang's joy was contagious.

Life was short. And it was sometimes filled with adversity. But look at this little dog. Nothing was too hard for him. Everything and everyone was worth his trouble. He had been to hell and back and was still singing the praises of life.

Tang was getting a second chance. Maybe *everyone* deserved a second chance.

Even Sarah.

CHAPTER 17

"He's all set," Joel said, returning from the back room and reentering the examining room with Tang in one arm. He looked so tiny and cute in his blue sweater, front paws draped over Joel's forearm and hindlimbs dangling. His face was all alight with happiness. It was time to go home.

"I don't know how to thank you, Joel."

"No need. It's my job." His smile was gracious but I could see behind the gaiety a weariness. He had been doing double shifts. I mustn't keep him. I hoped that Dr. Patali would soon recover and return to work.

"All set for Christmas?" he asked. "I'll bet Santa is going to be extra generous to you, little guy."

No doubt about it. Already most of the gifts under the tree were for him and, of course, the twins.

"Oh, yes. Just some last-minute things to finish

up. Hope you have a wonderful holiday too," I said. And I truly meant it. Even if it meant he was spending it with Sarah. But I mustn't ask. "I saw your stepdad, out in the waiting room."

Joel gave me a hopeful and very sincere look, which required a reply.

I obliged. "Thanks for setting the record straight."

"I thought Magnus should know that you had nothing to do with the rumors."

Joel knew exactly what I meant without my having to elaborate. Did he also know I was confused about him and Sarah?

"Magnus let Sarah go," I explained. "But I guess you know."

"I didn't," he said. "We don't mix business with personal issues. And Sarah's employment is definitely business. His."

And Joel's relationship with Sarah was none of mine. She was not a horrible person. Confused and ambitious, yes. But horrible? No. Everyone deserved love. I had learned that from this precious boy.

My humor returned as Joel handed Tang to me.

Outside, a gust of wind blew a smattering of crystals against the window.

"Oh-oh," Joel said. "Looks like the forecast is coming true. They're predicting an ice storm later today. It might be starting already. Good thing the hospital has emergency backup power. Except for a few staff to hold down the fort, we'll be shutting down early for Christmas Eve."

Who would have thought the clear blue sky could become overcast so quickly? Those wispy swirls of white I had noticed an hour ago were deceptive. They looked way too light to gather into storm clouds. And yet the day had grayed, the wind had grown and there was definitely some kind of precipitation falling from the sky.

We couldn't have been here for more than forty minutes. The sun had been shining so brightly and now this?

"I better go. Bruno is driving me and Tang back to Toronto. And we don't want to get stuck on the road."

"Drive safe. And hope to see you again."

I waited before answering, wondering if that was just an empty platitude. People always said things like 'I'll call you,' and never did.

"I'll text you some pictures," I suggested. And meant it.

"Please do. I'd love to see Tang under the Christmas tree."

At that moment I almost asked him to Christmas dinner. But his stepfather was here. In the waiting room, waiting for Joel to get off shift. They had plans.

I hoped they didn't plan to drive anywhere far. The roads were treacherous during an ice storm, and no amount of road salt could prevent all accidents.

Even as I held him, Tang's tail was thrashing against my leg. I set him down and hooked up his leash so that he could say goodbye to Joel.

The return trip was quick as we were headed in the opposite direction of rush hour. I pushed aside my visit with Joel. What was I expecting? He was at work. Tang was his patient. It was an inappropriate place and time to be spilling our guts. Besides, maybe Joel didn't have anything to spill.

Despite that, my mood was high. The future looked bright even if the day was turning out to be a little grim. But hey, it was only an ice storm. And provided we didn't end up in a twenty-car pileup I was happy. Exuberant, in fact. Tang was contentedly sleeping seat-belted beside me with his tongue folded under his chin and his head on my lap.

By the time we got back, the flurries had changed to ice pellets. Bruno dropped me off at Mom's. I wished him a Merry Christmas and told him Tang and I intended to drop by at his house on Boxing Day to give the family a gift.

"No. No gift necessary," he said. "Your company is all the family needs. Guilia and the girls can't wait to meet this little hero."

"I'll text you on Boxing Day for a convenient

time. Merry Christmas, Bruno." I reached around and kissed him on the cheek before getting out with Tang. "Our love to Guilia and the girls."

"*Buon Natale!*" Bruno drove off and we hurried through the ice and wind upstairs to the warmth, noise and cheer of Mom's condo.

We spent the afternoon preparing for tomorrow. There were last minute presents to wrap, baked goods to defrost. And oodles of food to prepare. Our giant turkey would be enough to feed twenty people.

The storm was raging in earnest by the time we sat down for Christmas Eve dinner. Jonny and Eva had checked out of their hotel and moved their luggage into the spare bedroom. The kids were going to sleep on mattresses on the floor. Not because there wasn't a spare bedroom for them, but because it was tradition for Christmas Eve. The house was becoming a joyous muddle of scattered bedding, winter coats and boots and towels for wiping wet feet.

Tomorrow the ice storm should be over. I hoped Bruno had made it home before the worst of it arrived. And what about Joel and Mr. Hancock? Would they have stayed overnight in Guelph or returned to Toronto where Joel lived? I was so tempted to text and ask if they were all right.

I didn't.

As I sat in the warm living room with Tang and my niece and nephew playing on the floor away from the gas fireplace, my mom and Eva busy in the kitchen, and Jonny searching the streaming services for yet one more Christmas movie, I felt relaxed, content and safe.

I noticed that Jonny was wearing a fisherman knit sweater.

"Where did you get that?" I asked. "I've never seen you in a crewneck before. You hate them."

He glanced down from where he was busily clicking on the remote, scrolling through the listings. "Oh, this? Eva's mom gave it to me last year."

That explained why he was wearing it. I was probably the only one who knew he hated crewnecks.

He laid down the remote and tugged at the crewneck. The reason he didn't like the style was because he felt they itched. But Jonny being Jonny would do anything to please his wife. "Oh, by the way. I ran into your assistant the other day."

Former assistant. But why would he know that? I'd had no time to get him up to speed on my professional gaffs. And now would spoil the mood.

"You mean Sarah?" I said.

"Yeah. It was at the—"

St. Lawrence Market. A thunderbolt of comprehension hit me. That wasn't Joel I saw at the market, it was Jonny!

"Why did you buy her a coffee?"

"What? How did you know… Oh, she told you."

No, she didn't.

"Uh, never mind." What did it matter? It wasn't Joel! I had introduced Jonny to Sarah once, months ago, and knowing Sarah, her outgoing personality had made her stop and speak to Jonny when she recognized him at the market.

A deep contentment settled over me. Jonny returned to his listings, and I to my daydreams.

Outside the frost-rimmed glass doors I watched the crystal droplets cling like sugar to the rooftop patio rails, the aluminum frames of the furniture and the potted trees. The strings of white lights that Jonny and the kids had strung this morning looked like textured strip lighting, and millions of frozen drops clung to the pergola overhead. The scene had a powerful effect and I was grateful to be safe and warm and surrounded by my loved ones.

The wonderful smells of cooking and baking and the luscious eggnog in my hand made me want to hang onto this moment forever. Nothing was better than this. Nothing!

Suddenly the room went dark.

"What happened?" Eva called from the kitchen.

"Power went out," Jonny said.

He was looking out the window. None of the surrounding houses had power.

"Oh, no. What are were going to do about the food?" Eva asked.

"Don't worry," Mom replied. "This building has a backup generator for situations like this. The electricity should be back any minute."

CHAPTER 18

Christmas day dawned brilliant and clear. The storm had stopped somewhere between midnight and dawn. The kids were up with the sun and we had opened presents and messed up the house with festive gift bags, wrapping paper, ribbons and bows and sticky scotch tape. And hot apple cider glasses with cinnamon sticks.

Breakfast was really a very late brunch made up of French toast with maple syrup, chocolatey croissants, buttery blueberry muffins and scrambled eggs with smoked salmon. And a giant bowl of fruit salad. Hot chocolate for the twins and fragrant freshly ground coffee for the adults.

Tis the season.

Today would be spent cleaning house and preparing Christmas dinner. But first things first. It occurred to me that Bruno's family may not have been as lucky as us to have backup power.

I called him on his cellphone and he answered after five rings.

"*Buon Natale*, Bruno," I said. "Hope Santa was good to you."

"Oh, very good," he said. "I now have socks with reindeers on them."

I laughed. "Adorable. You must wear them when I see you."

"That might be a problem, Mari. We lost power last night and it has not returned. On the news it says we might be without power for a day or two."

"You mean you won't have electricity to make your Christmas dinner?"

"No. But we will manage."

"But you can't stay at your place without heat!"

"We have big winter coats and plenty of blankets."

"No. You must come—"

I dug in my heels, called to my mother, and quickly explained the situation to her.

"No question they must come here for Christmas dinner," she said.

He overheard and replied, "Ah, we cannot impose. There are four of us. Too many. And we do not even know your *mamma*."

"Well, she knows you. I told her all about you, and how kind you have been to me and Tang. So, we won't take no for an answer. Mom's place is huge. There's plenty of room. Please Bruno. Don't make me steal a car and come and get you."

At this point Mom grabbed a towel, wiped her hands that were sticky with stuffing and took the phone from me. "Bruno, this is Elizabeth, Mari's mother. If you don't bring your family over. I will come and fetch you myself."

He laughed. "All right. And our dog? She is welcome too?"

"Are you kidding? Tang will be beside himself to have a doggie friend. We'll be expecting her." Mom handed the phone back to me and returned to stuffing her turkey.

"It's set then?" I asked.

"It is. See you at what time?"

"Any time that is convenient for you. Dinner is at six o'clock, kid's time. But come any time before that."

He understood perfectly. If children were not fed by that time, they turned into cookie monsters. "See you before six."

I went back into the living room where Eva and Jonny were cramming crumpled gift wrap into a large, black, plastic garbage bag. It was already three p.m. Time to vacuum and start setting the table. The turkey would be in the oven soon, and Eva returned to the kitchen to start working on the vegetables.

"I need a potato peeler," Mom shouted.

"I'll do it," Jonny said and dropped the garbage bag in front of me to take a vegetable peeler from the kitchen drawer.

That left me on cleanup and garbage detail.

When my work was done, the condo smelled like roast turkey and homemade cranberry sauce and pumpkin pie. It was a homey but heavenly smell. The sun had set, what little sun there had been, and everything was freezing up outside once more.

"I'm taking Tang out for a short walk before dinner," I said. "Don't forget to let Bruno and his family in when they arrive. I should be home before they get here."

I pulled on Tang's black rubber boots to protect his feet from the icy streets and his sweater to shield him from the cold. I worried about his tongue freezing with it hanging out like that. But Joel had told me not to worry. It wouldn't freeze. As long as we didn't stay outside too long.

We left the condo and descended to the lobby, where a beautiful Christmas tree stood alone all decked out in traditional colors of red, blue, white, yellow and green. The lights from the building illuminated the street and the lampposts remained unlit. Most of the buildings were dark but some, like Mom's, had backup power. So, there was light to see by.

"Come on, sweetie," I said as we exited the warmth of the lobby and was slapped by cold air. Fortunately, there was no wind. A gentle drift of ice crystals floated down to greet us. "We won't go far. Just across the street to the park so you can do your business."

I wanted to show him the Nativity scene in the niche of frozen trees.

It was all lit up. How strange. The power outage had not affected the Nativity scene.

There were the three wise men. The shepherds with their flocks of sheep. The virgin Mary and her husband Joseph. And in a bed of hay, the baby Jesus. All encompassed in a halo of light.

Tang trundled over to the manger and stared at the interesting figures. They weren't moving so he nudged one or two with his nose.

"They aren't real, sweetie," I said.

Tang moseyed up to the baby Jesus and lifted his head. Out of his mouth came a howl of joy. I laughed until I was almost crying.

"I thought that was you," a voice said.

I swung around in shock and came face to face with Joel.

"Hi Marilee."

"Joel! What are you doing here?"

"Magnus and I were driving by and I saw you and Tang come out of that building there and go into the park. I had a notion to follow you."

"Why?"

He shrugged. "I don't know. I just feel like something isn't finished with us."

What a strange thing to say. I felt the same way, but was hesitant to respond. Instead, I asked, "Where's Magnus?"

"He's in the car."

"You left him in the car?"

"He's okay. He suggested I catch up with you."

That was odd. Mr. Hancock thought there was something between me and Joel? Mr. Hancock never struck me as the type of person who noticed human emotions. Behaviors, yes. He was cued into people's actions and reactions. That was how he knew how to respond to get the results he wanted. It was different for me. I was in sales. Selling was all about emotion.

"Why?" I asked. "Why did he want you to catch up with me?"

"He thinks there's something between us."

Silence and the tinkle of ice-coated leaves. Even though I now knew that it wasn't Joel who had met Sarah at the market, I was cautious.

"Please, Mari," Joel said, his breath puffing with the cold. "Just say what's on your mind."

One thing I had to say for Joel, he was always direct. I opened my mouth, then shut it, then opened it again. "I thought there was something going on with you and Sarah."

"What? Where did you get an idea like that?"

"You took her out for dinner in Vancouver."

"I did? That's news to me."

"You mean, you didn't?"

"No, I didn't. How could I possibly have had the time? And even if I'd had the time, why would I do that? We had a quick coffee. That was all." He paused. "How could there be anything between us. I only met her at the Christmas party and then went with her for coffee afterwards. It was really late too, but she insisted on it. I only did that because I knew she was your assistant and I thought if I had a coffee with her, I might get to see you again."

Oh wow.

"But we met on the plane."

"Yes, we did. I had no way of knowing that was going to happen. Had I known, I would have forgone the coffee." He gave me his wicked smile. And I melted.

"I'm sorry, Joel. I'm... I'm caught off-guard. I don't know what to say."

"Say you'll reserve a day we can spend together before you fly back to Vancouver."

That idea now seemed kind of alien to me. I had no job to return to. What reason did I have to go back to Vancouver?

"Uh." I was stupidly speechless.

"Look, you're freezing." I was. I wore a black felt bowler hat and a vintage wool coat with red ribbons and big black buttons when I should have put on my doggie jacket, the pale blue, puffy parka. But hey, it was Christmas and I was being festive.

"You look really beautiful, by the way."

Beautiful? *Me?*

"So, is it a date?"

"Um. Yes?"

"You make that sound like a question."

"That's because I do have a question." Long pause. "Where were you going just now?"

"Ah, Magnus and I were looking for a restaurant that still had power, and that was open on Christmas night. Likely Chinese food."

"You can't do that. You can't eat at a restaurant on Christmas. You have to come to my mom's place. It's just across the street. Come. Let's get Magnus and go now before we freeze to death."

My phone suddenly rang and I tugged it out of my pocket.

Oh dear. It was Sarah.

I almost clicked my phone off. My hand started towards my pocket. Why would I want to speak to her? I didn't. But curiosity got the best of me.

"Excuse me for a moment, Joel. I'll meet you at your car." I could see the solitary vehicle from where I stood.

"No problem. I'll be waiting."

I waited until Joel had turned his back, then I removed my black wool mittens and slid the phone open. It took a few tries before the cold phone responded to my stiff finger. Then I raised it to my ear. "Sarah?"

"Oh, Marilee." She stifled a sob.

She was crying. Why?

"What's the matter? What's happened?"

"I'm stuck at the airport. The ice storm has grounded all flights from Toronto until after Boxing Day. The hotels around here are all booked up. I've got nowhere to go!"

How did she guess I knew she was in Toronto? Then it occurred to me that it wasn't a guess. Although I thought I had dodged her, she had seen me that day I spotted her at the market. Why didn't she say anything? She was having coffee with my brother!

And she had followed Joel to Toronto for the holidays. Had she approached him? Did he even know she was here?

"Marilee. Are you there? I need your help."

She needed my help? What I really wanted to do was snipe at her. *What do you want me to do about it?*

"I—I tried to see Joel." She burst into sobs again.

It amazed me how spontaneous Sarah could be. Was that a trait of her generation? Or was it just her? Who did that? Who just bought a plane ticket on the spur of the moment. To pursue a guy she'd just met?

And yet, that was the attitude it took to be successful in big business.

Every bone in my body wanted to hang up on her. She had created this situation all by herself. Why should I help her?

"What happened," I asked.

"He said there was someone else."

I sighed. How could she know I was interested in Joel? I never told her. And yet I felt like she had stabbed me in the back once more.

I knew what I had to do. I couldn't leave her

stranded at the airport.

"Stop crying, Sarah. You have somewhere to go."

CHAPTER 19

The condo was crowded when I returned with Tang and Joel and his stepfather. Bruno was already there with his family. We greeted everyone and I made introductions.

"This is Joel, the wonderful surgeon that saved Tang's life. And his stepfather Magnus Hancock." I decided not to elaborate by mentioning that Mr. Hancock was my former boss. That would mean an explanation of why he was no longer my employer and I refused to subject him to that kind of embarrassment. It was Christmas after all!

Bruno introduced his wife Guilia. The twins Mia and Michael had already introduced themselves to Bruno's girls Bianca and Aurora, and were showing off all the new toys that Santa had brought them. Tang was very pleased to meet their golden retriever, Luna. They were sniffing each other and wagging tails. The equivalent of a human handshake.

"Mom, can I borrow your car?" I asked as Jonny led the men away to unburden themselves of their winter gear. I hadn't bothered to remove my coat or boots.

"Are you crazy? Where do you think you're going?" She grabbed the black felt hat off my head and the mitts I was clutching to my chest.

"I have to pick Sarah up at the airport. She's stranded." I unhooked Tang from his harness and leash, and he shook himself out. "And please set another plate. I invited her for Christmas dinner too."

Joel overheard me and came over from being relieved of his coat and boots by Jonny. "I'll come with you. I'll drive. I'll borrow Magnus's car."

"It's treacherous out there," Mom said. "Can't Sarah take a cab?" By this time, Sarah had become a household name and everyone knew who she was.

"There are no cabs," I said. "They're overbooked because of last night's storm. The roads are slick and still covered in ice."

"All the more reason you shouldn't go."

"I can't just abandon her."

"Actually, you can," Joel said. "But you won't. You're an amazing person, Mari. That's why *I'll* go."

"Do you have studded tires?" Bruno asked, approaching us unexpectedly. He too had overheard Sarah's predicament and wished to help.

Joe shook his head. "No. I believe they are regular winter tires. Aren't they, Magnus?" Mr.

Hancock nodded from behind him.

"Then you shouldn't be driving on the ice. It's not safe. I will go."

I grabbed him by the arm. "No. Bruno. You just got here."

"I will go. I insist. It is the least I can do for you. You have taken in my family. Besides, I have studded tires on my cab. I will be perfectly safe."

"Then I must go with you."

"That isn't necessary. You have all these guests here, and Guilia would like to get to know you. And there is this young man who I know is dying to spend some time with you." He winked at Joel.

"No argument from me," Joel said.

"But..." Sarah was my problem. It was a huge imposition to ask Bruno to pick her up at the airport. "You don't know Sarah. You don't know what she looks like."

"Describe her to me. Write her name on a card. I will flash it. And she will come to me. But phone her as well, so that she knows I am coming."

Finally, I agreed. Bruno was one in a million.

Outside on the frozen patio the outdoor lamps and festive twinkle lights gleamed bright. Because of the building's generators the exterior seating area was filled with a warm glow. The gas firepit blazed away. There were wool blankets and pillows on the cushions for people to cuddle up with while Mom, Eva and Jonny served hot drinks and appetizers. I should be helping too, but Mr. Hancock suddenly moved over to where Joel and I stood by the glass rail overlooking the park.

"Joel, would you mind if I spoke to Marilee in private for a moment?"

Joel glanced at me and I nodded. Whatever Mr. Hancock had to say was best got out of the way so that we could all enjoy the evening.

"Be my guest." Joel nodded encouragingly at me, and stepped away to join the others by the fire.

I smiled at my former boss. I felt no antagonism towards him.

He smiled back. "I really am sorry for all the pain I've caused you."

"It wasn't your fault."

"I believe it was… Nevertheless, I apologize, and I would like to offer you your job back with a raise in pay. And a promotion. To Chief Marketing Officer."

A promotion? When I thought back to how much stress there was involved in being an executive, I realized something. I didn't want another promotion. I had already been promoted. Twice. And they had not made me any happier. More was not always better. More meant more responsibilities, more obligations and more people to account to. A promotion to CMO would just pile on and I would no longer own my life. I wanted something different.

Mr. Hancock was waiting for my response. This quietness was the last thing he had hoped for. But any way I turned it about in my head, the outcome was the same. I wanted to spend more time with my dog and the people that I loved.

This was going to be awkward. It must have been difficult for him to humble himself for me, and now, here I was about to disappoint him.

I shook my head. "It is my turn to apologize," I said. "That is a very generous offer. I have learned so much working for your company and I appreciate all the wonderful opportunities you have provided me. But... I've had time to think about what I'm doing with my life. And I've come to a revelation... Life is too short. I think—no—I know that I don't want to spend it that way. I've decided to do something else with my days."

Mr. Hancock's brows rose. His expression wasn't disappointment, anger or anything negative. It was simple curiosity. "What kind of thing?"

I felt strong and confident for the first time since I learned of Tang's cancer. "I want to open a pet shop of my own."

His eyes widened further, and then a look of total comprehension smoothed away all the tension in his face. He could not be more pleased for me. "I love that idea."

"So do I," Joel said approaching us with two glasses of wine. "Sorry for eavesdropping."

"Don't apologize," I said, accepting a glass. "I was going to tell you anyway."

The other glass went to Joel's stepfather. Mr. Hancock seemed to cue in that this was a moment we wished to ourselves. He wasn't wrong. He wished us well, excused himself and joined my mom. She had just come outside with a platter of cranberry brie tarts and tempted him with the goodies.

"I think they might just hit it off," I giggled.

"Nothing would please me more."

"Joel?"

"Yes, Mari."

My eyes wandered to the snowy landscape below us, past the aluminum rail with its glass panes. The park had the feel of a Winter Wonderland. Surrounded by darkness, starlight illumined the scene making the ice crystals in the trees sparkle like diamonds. In the center of the park in a niche of frozen trees, the Nativity scene glowed with a surreal light.

"What would you think if I decided to stay here in Toronto?"

Joel's gaze took on a warm, soft appeal. "I would say, that is the thing that would please me more than your mom and my stepdad getting together."

He lowered his head and planted a gentle kiss on my lips. Before anything further could develop, I heard the sliding doors open.

Jonny came onto the patio accompanied by

Sarah and Bruno. Thank goodness they were back safely.

Sarah saw Joel holding my hand and Mr. Hancock stared across the flagstones from the firepit frowning at her. The moment lasted less than a few seconds, and then all of the tension in his body seemed to fade away. Mr. Hancock strolled over, good humor restored, and said, "Merry Christmas, Sarah."

She stood awkwardly. For the first time unsure of herself.

His encouraging attitude allowed her to relax, just as he had. And she wished him the same before he turned and went indoors to see if my mom needed help.

I forced my attention back to Sarah and asked if she would like a drink. Before she answered, I saw that one of her hands was fiddling nervously at her ear. She felt strange and uncomfortable and guilty. And with good reason.

Tang trundled up to her in his blue sweater with a red bow around his neck and gave her an explosive happy bark.

She laughed, and so did we all. Each and every one of us who were still outside had turned at the sound.

"Merry Christmas everyone," Sarah said, and glanced down at her boots. "Especially you, little man." And they returned her greeting just before Mom opened the sliding door to call everyone inside.

They began to migrate indoors until I was left alone with Sarah, and little Tang waiting at our feet. It was bitterly cold and we both clutched at the collars of our coats. Dinner was almost ready.

Mom flashed me five fingers through the window, meaning dinner would be ready in five minutes.

Sarah gazed at me and saw that my eyes had returned to her face. Hanging from her earlobes were my Silver Bell earrings. I wasn't going to make a scene over them. And I no longer wished to rip them off her ears.

She quickly began to remove them, but I stopped her. "Keep them," I said. "As a Christmas present."

"But I have nothing for you."

I smiled. She had no idea. If it wasn't for her, I may never have thought to change course and see what was really important in life.

Through the glass doors I watched my family and friends. Mom and Eva in the dining room setting food on the table; Mr. Hancock helping. What an unusual sight!

Jonny opening a bottle of wine and Bruno lighting candles, while Guilia helped with the glasses and beverages for the children. Michael and Mia played on the floor with their newfound friends. And Joel had moved to the fireplace where Luna was lying by the warmth and comfort of the fire. Joel's head lifted from petting the dog. And our eyes met through the glass. Joel raised his wineglass to me. And Tang stared adoringly up at Sarah.

"Merry Christmas, Sarah," I said, scooping Tang up into my arms. "Let's go inside. It looks like the Christmas feast is about to begin."

When everything goes wrong, and things seem like they can't get any worse, Tang looks up into the heavens and sings because to live is to love, and there is nothing better in life than love.

Joy to the world, little man. And God bless you!

Books by Daphne Lynn Stewart:

All She Wants for Christmas
All NYC publicist Belle Rice and her best friend, bestselling romance author Cate Zarcova, want is to re-experience the white Christmas of their childhood in a quiet countryside estate. When Belle rescues a runaway dog and returns it to its owner Christopher Winters, cupid strikes and Belle falls hard, not only for Chris but also for the little dog. Only one thing impedes her happiness. Chris is a recent widow, with a new girlfriend.

http://www.amazon.com/All-She-Wants-Christmas-lovers-ebook/dp/B00QMTZURQ/

Christmas in June
Leigh and Matthew were best friends who met at her grandmother's lakeside cottage in a charming tourist town every Christmas. They dated through high school and fifteen years later Leigh is a reporter and Matt owns the Little Inn at Bayfield. Leigh plans to advertise Christmas in Bayfield via a documentary. Her attraction to Matt is rekindled even though he has a fiancée and she a boyfriend. Just when she thinks she has managed to shield her heart from him and her current boyfriend, her docudrama, which is nothing short of Reality TV, shows her and the rest of the world the truth.

http://www.amazon.com/Christmas-June-lovers-Bright-Romance-ebook/dp/B010MQQYJC

The Christmas Mix-up
On the eve of the Christmas season Danica Meriweather picks up the wrong pet carrier at her local airport, and meets the man of her dreams. Only thing is: she never really saw his face. Now she has *his* dog, and their plan to exchange pets is postponed due to a raging snowstorm. Love blossoms nonetheless even though they have only communicated by phone. Meanwhile Danica's catering business, which is run from her home—a heritage building—is threatened to be torn down by a ruthless corporation. Her only hope is to convince the company's CEO the value of historic homes. She agrees to cater his corporate Christmas party despite mixed feelings, and soon learns why her feelings are mixed.

http://www.amazon.com/Christmas-Mix-Up-lovers-Bright-Romance-ebook/dp/B0116H9IF8

The Christmas Bunny
Kendra Tyler has big dreams, one of which includes becoming a professor of animal behavior. To accomplish her dream, she must go to grad school, and to pay for school she needs a good part-time job. This she finds at the Bunny Club. Her other dream is to marry the wonderful man she's dating. Cabe Alexander. She must keep Cabe from finding out what she really does for a living. As Christmas approaches and her secret is exposed, Kendra is betrayed by the man she trusts and finds help and love from a most unlikely source. Another man,

Nicholas Marley is waiting on the sidelines to shake up her destiny.

http://www.amazon.com/Christmas-Bunny-lovers-Bright-Romance-ebook/dp/B016E7VRG8

Dashing Through The Snow
When Chelsea Doll meets Jason Frost she realizes she is engaged to the wrong brother. She and Bryce are planning their Christmas Eve wedding at Langdon Hall a luxury country estate hotel. It seems she and Bryce's brother have everything in common including a love of dogs. If only she had met him first.

https://www.amazon.com/Dashing-Through-Snow-lovers-Romance-ebook/dp/B01I1V7JQ2?ie=UTF8&*Version*=1&*entries*=0#nav-subnav

A Very Catty Christmas
Budding artist Lorelei Channing is in love with art curator Harry Snowden. But he doesn't know she exists. By day she is Lori Channing, a docent at the Art Gallery of Hamilton; by night she is textile artiste *Lorelei*. Due to a mixup, Lorelei has won a contest to have one of her pieces in a prestigious art show, that opens on Christmas Eve. Her cat keeps escaping and wreaking havoc in the museum shop. But because museum docents are volunteers, the CEO cannot fire her. When Harry finally notices her, he still doesn't know she is the bumbling docent the CEO complains of. Between Lori's mistakes and her cat's mischief the CEO

begins suspect and Lorelei starts to wonder if she's dating the right man.

https://www.amazon.com/Very-Catty-Christmas-lovers-Romance-ebook/dp/B01IAKI6IY?ie=UTF8&*Version*=1&*entries*=0

Rocky Mountain Christmas
What would you do if you fell in love with your cousin's boyfriend? Joy Zamboni is a magazine writer for a rag called Cats and Dogs. Her Christmas assignment? To write an article on how dogs are replacing men in the loves of modern women. To aid in her research she adopts an Australian shepherd dog. Rocky is skittish on their first outing and runs halfway down the block. Then out of nowhere, a dashing fellow appears and shows Joy how to win the dog's confidence. Jack owns a canine training school, and they hit it off. When Joy and Rocky arrive at her father's mountain lodge, her dear cousin Ellie is there with her boyfriend—Jack.

https://www.amazon.com/Rocky-Mountain-Christmas-lovers-Romance-ebook/dp/B01ICBESP6?ie=UTF8&*Version*=1&*entries*=0

Christmastime in the City
Romance bookstore owner, Olivia Snow, has a serious choice to make. When the godlike sous-chef at the French bistro next door saves her cat Nilly from the top of a lamppost in the quaint town of Dundas, Olivia believes her months-old feud with him is over. She has feelings for him

until her younger sister Gabrielle beats her to the punch. They both need dates for their cousin Darla's Christmas wedding at a gorgeous chateau near Paris. A castle wedding is a dream-come-true. When sister Gabby steals her date, Olivia is desperate to find another and settles for Hank a wine connoisseur and manager of her local liquor store. Yeah, pretty ordinary guy, she thinks, but boy is she ever wrong!

https://www.amazon.com/Christmastime-City-lovers-Bright-Romance-ebook/dp/B07GZ44PY9/ref=sr_1_3?s=digital-text&ie=UTF8&qid=1538593605&sr=1-3

Mistletoe Inn
Laurel Westlake is furious when winery owner Tom Holiday almost runs over her sweet little dogs Bella and Daisy in an icy hotel parking lot in the lakeshore town of Niagara-on-the-lake. The hotel can't take her because of a burst water main. Now she's late for a meeting with an important client. She is to plan a Christmas party for a big time realtor. Worse, as she's leaving, she crashes her car into a crate of expensive wine Tom is unloading. She's frustrated, he's mad, but when she injures herself on a piece of bottle glass Tom shows true compassion. She could fall for him, but he's already dating someone else. Someone from her past…

https://www.amazon.com/Mistletoe-Inn-Lovers-Bright-Romance-ebook/dp/B07GZ7YXMJ/ref=sr_1_2?s=digital-text&ie=UTF8&qid=1538595420&sr=1-2

Let it Snow
It's love at first sight on a snowy winter's day in early December when Joe Douglas and Noelle Hollyburn meet at her cousin's veterinary practice in Ottawa. Noelle is a pet photographer. Joe's dog has peed on her and she has to change out of her soiled clothing and wear her cousin Nicola's lab coat. It just happens to have the name Dr. Nicola Hollyburn stitched on it. When Wealthy advertising executive Joe Douglas arrives to pick up his bulldog, Bosco, he mistakes Noelle for Nicola, the vet. Joe asks her on a date. At Noelle's pleading, Nicola agrees to allow Noelle to pretend to be her. It's too late for Noelle to correct him now that they are dating, but her luck can only last so long before he finds out who she really is.

https://www.amazon.com/Let-Snow-Lovers-Bright-Romance-ebook/dp/B07GZM16SZ/ref=sr_1_1?s=digital-text&ie=UTF8&qid=1538595420&sr=1-1

It Wouldn't be Christmas Without You
When Abby Hollybrook's high school crush Max Granger returns at Christmas with two dogs he needs to rehome, Abby knows that the troublesome pups are about to change her life. Her landlady hates the dogs and she hates Abby. Fortunately, she doesn't hate Max. Max's rented house no longer allows dogs and Abby's landlady jumps at the chance to find him a new place—preferably by her side. Abby must keep her rescue center open and

train Max's dogs. But will it be enough? Will Abby and Max get together by Christmas or will Abby's landlady force them apart?

https://www.amazon.com/Wouldnt-Christmas-Without-You-Romance-ebook/dp/B08PN6QGZK/ref=sr_1_5?dchild=1&qid=1620419777&refinements=p_27%3ADaphne+Lynn+Stewart&s=digital-text&sr=1-5&text=Daphne+Lynn+Stewart

Three Nights Before Christmas

After accidentally pepper spraying herself *and* her fiancé's dog in a cooking accident, Sophie Star has a nightmare that her engagement ring cracks in half. The next morning couldn't get any worse. When she takes the dog to the vet she discovers that he is her high school boyfriend. And when she goes to see the eye doctor he happens to be ex number two. To top it off, ex number three turns out to be her parents' contractor! Are these blasts from the past warning her not to marry Charlie? Or do they have something to do with a dog she can't remember but loved as a child?

https://www.amazon.com/Three-Nights-Before-Christmas-Romance-ebook/dp/B094DXZ6DB/ref=sr_1_1?dchild=1&qid=1620672201&refinements=p_27%3ADaphne+Lynn+Stewart&s=digital-text&sr=1-1&text=Daphne+Lynn+Stewart

The Christmas Castle

Julie Bramblea's estranged grandfather died leaving her a Gothic castle and a mystery to solve. Why did her mother run away to marry Julie's father and never reconnect with her family again? When her cat Shakespeare goes missing all of the pieces start to fall into place as she falls for her newly retained lawyer and his little boy.

https://www.amazon.com/Christmas-Castle-lovers-Bright-Romance-ebook/dp/B094NW94ST/ref=sr_1_1?dchild=1&keywords=The+Christmas+Castle+Daphne+Lynn+Stewart&qid=1631651476&s=digital-text&sr=1-1

Christmas in September
When April Snow meets Sam Fir and his teenaged daughter, she learns that love is synonymous with 'home.' Lifestyle journalist April is assigned to pen an article plugging Sam's new mashup business, a coffeehouse/art gallery/bookshop. Instead, she finds herself in a game of deception where she helps Sam's daughter hide the fact that she is keeping a dog in their condo without his knowledge. Will this destroy April's chances at romance with Sam or can she help make a young girl happy without jeopardizing her relationship with the father?

https://www.amazon.com/Christmas-September-lovers-Bright-Romance-ebook/dp/B0BMWBYDTX?ref_=ast_author_dp

SUMMER DESTINY ROMANCE SERIES:

Paradise on Deck: A Summer Destiny Romance

Do you believe in destiny? Ariel Stone does not until she meets handsome deck and landscape designer Ben Hammer on a cruise ship. Ariel is aboard the *Crystal Serenity* redecorating one of their exclusive penthouse suites when she experiences a decorating emergency. Ben comes to the rescue, but refuses payment for the job so she invites him to join her for a drink. They promise not to tell each other anything about their personal lives, and instead play a 'game' that Ben calls Destiny.

https://www.amazon.com/Paradise-Deck-Summer-Destiny-Romance-ebook/dp/B01IE0IVB2/ref=sr_1_3?s=digital-text&ie=UTF8&qid=1473184274&sr=1-3#nav-subnav

If Not For You: A Summer Destiny Romance

When a man loves a woman he will go to any extent to win her, but to what extent will he go to save her life? Leanne Constance meets Andy Briggs at a psychology conference in L.A. They hit it off and spend one night together in a luxurious room at the Beverly Hills hotel, where her most precious memory is having breakfast with him on their bougainvillea-draped patio. One thing stands in the way of happily ever after. Leanne has a secret, a serious health condition. When Andy discovers her secret, he is horrified that he might lose her. Can he save her, and if he does, at what cost?

https://www.amazon.com/If-Not-You-Destiny-Romance-ebook/dp/B01M1EDZ2R/ref=sr_1_1?s=digital-text&ie=UTF8&qid=1473857825&sr=1-1#nav-subnav

Author's Note

Based on a true story. The real-life story took place around Christmastime 2014. This version of "Tang's Christmas Miracle" is fiction, so none of the characters are real. Except Tang.

Tang is a shih-poo who developed cancer in his lower jaw when he was five years old. He was saved by the veterinarians at the Ontario Veterinary College hospital. After a surgical cure, he went on to live for ten more years, never failing to show his love and appreciation of everything that lives. His happy bark will long be remembered.

About the Author

Christmas is my favourite time of year, because that is when I found my "forever guy," and so I will always equate Christmas with love. Most of my stories take place during the festive season, sometimes in small towns and sometimes in the big city, and everything is always Merry and Bright (although it may not start out that way) and love and happiness are possible for anyone.

I am mainly a novelist but have also written heartwarming stories for the popular series Chicken Soup for the Soul under the name of Deborah Cannon. You can read the non-fiction version of "Tang's Christmas Miracle" in CHRISTMAS IN CANADA and "Our Yard: A Canadian Tale" in THE SPIRIT OF CANADA.

I currently have two series. So, on your summer holidays, stretch out in your backyard or on the beach, pour yourself a cool glass of wine and indulge in a SUMMER DESTINY romance. As autumn fades to winter cuddle up with your fur baby by a roaring fire on a cold day with a cup of hot cocoa and enjoy one of my cosy MERRY AND BRIGHT holiday love stories.

For anyone who is curious as to who those cute pets are on the covers of my Christmas romances, they are all pets of either my friends or my family. So those cuties are real! Sadly, some have passed away now. My precious Ming and Tang are gone, but I leave these love stories as a legacy to my beloved dogs.